# The OUTCASTS

ANNE SCHRAFF

URBAN UNDERGROUND®

A Boy Called Twister
Dark Secrets
Deliverance
Don't Think About Tomorrow
The Fairest
If You Really Loved Me
Leap of Faith
Like a Broken Doll
The Lost
No Fear
One of Us
**The Outcasts**
Out of Love for You
Outrunning the Darkness
The Quality of Mercy
See No Evil
Shadows of Guilt
The Stranger
Time of Courage
To Be a Man
To Catch a Dream
The Rescuers
The Unforgiven
The Water's Edge
Wildflower

ISBN-13: 978-1-61651-662-8
ISBN-10: 1-61651-662-3
eBook: 978-1-61247-356-7

Printed in Guangzhou, China
1011/CA21101701

17 16 15 14 13    1 2 3 4 5

# CHAPTER ONE

It was the first day of school at Harriet Tubman High School. "Hey, Sereeta," Marko Lane called out, "Your mom on the wagon yet?" Olivia Manley, Sereeta's mother, had shown up at the school very drunk. She had had to be half carried to her door by Jaris Spain and his girlfriend, Sereeta.

Sereeta Prince and her good friend Sami Archer were walking onto the campus for morning classes. Sami yelled back at Marko, "Hey fool, you a senior now. Act like one. Whatsa matter with you, sucka? You almost a man, and you acting like a mean little kid. You better grow up quick, dog, or somebody gonna knock you down."

"Ooooo, I scared!" Marko crowed, laughing. "Maybe you weigh more than the half back on our football team, girl. But I'm not afraid of you. You still hit like a girl!"

Sami stopped and put her hands on her hips. She glared at Marko and declared, "Dog, you got lotsa enemies around this school. Know why? 'Cause you talkin' trash all the time. You turn up dead in an alley, the cops'd have to question half the school."

"Just ignore him," Sereeta advised, a pained look on her face. "He's attracted to blood like a shark."

Sereeta only hoped Marko didn't know about what happened the other night. There was a party at the Manley home. Sereeta's stepfather, Perry, and her mother were on the front lawn, arguing loudly. They got so loud so late at night that the neighbors complained and the police were called.

Jaris Spain had not yet arrived at Tubman to begin his senior year. He was later than the rest because he was driving his fourteen-year-old sister, Chelsea. She was beginning her freshman year. And she was taking a long time getting dressed for the important occasion.

When Chelsea finally appeared, Lorenzo Spain, her father, checked her out. "Nice. Very nice," he commented. "Cute little top. Nice jeans. You look good, little girl. Jaris, he done a fine job of helping you pick out your stuff."

"Everything is too big," Chelsea complained. "It's all a size too big. Everybody's gonna laugh at me."

"You look fine, baby," Pop assured her. "Beautiful. Ain't she a picture, Monie?"

"Yes," Monica Spain agreed. "You look lovely, Chelsea. Now have a wonderful first day at Tubman."

Chelsea followed her brother to his Honda Civic. "I'm so nervous," she confessed. "I don't know any of the teachers, except for Ms. Colbert for science. I'm sure glad I got involved in that opossum rescue program with Shadrach. Otherwise, I wouldn't even know Ms. Colbert. Athena and Inessa and I have about the same class schedules. That's good. Then I got a class that Maurice and Heston are in. And there's one class with Keisha—"

"Good, good," Jaris interrupted. "Come on, chili pepper, it's getting late." He didn't want to be late for his first senior class. Chelsea would have preferred to ride her bike or walk to school. But she'd gotten involved in some trouble, and she was grounded. Now Jaris was stuck with taking her everywhere.

It had taken Jaris two minutes to pull his T-shirt over his head and put on his jeans. Now he drummed his fingers and stared at the kitchen clock. Chelsea primped, brushed her hair, checked and rechecked what she was wearing. Finally, they were getting into the car.

Chelsea hesitated at the car door, "Jaris, this top looks okay with the jeans, doesn't it? I mean, is orangey orange really a good color for me?" she asked.

"It's perfect, smashing!" Jaris declared, getting behind the wheel. "I've never seen such a great combination as those jeans and that orange top." Jaris was getting to sound more and more like Pop when he was exasperated.

The Honda rolled from the driveway and headed for Tubman. Jaris hoped he'd find a parking spot closer than a half mile from the classrooms. If you arrived late, you had to park at the outer edge of the parking lot.

Jaris circled around and finally found a spot. "We gotta run," Jaris told his sister.

"There's Athena," Chelsea cried happily. She began waving frantically. "Hi, Athena! Do you think she sees me, Jaris?"

"Yeah, yeah," Jaris assured her. "She sees you. I can tell." Jaris knew his teachers more or less. But he knew little about a teacher named Langston Myers. He had been named for the great African-American poet, Langston Hughes. Myers was an aspiring writer too. He'd had a few poems published, and he was shopping his first novel around to publishers. At forty-seven years of age, Mr. Myers was worried that perhaps he wouldn't make his mark in the world as his namesake had. He feared having to remain forever teaching senior English at Tubman High School.

English class was right after lunch. The teacher printed his name on the blackboard. Then he took a roll call and assigned seats. Finally, he handed out sheets on the grading system. Some students had questions. Mr. Myers answered curtly in his deep baritone voice. As the teacher did all this, Jaris studied him. Mr. Myers was a tall, dark-skinned man with thinning hair and piercing eyes. He looked and acted like someone you wouldn't want to tangle with.

"Good afternoon, ladies and gentlemen," he began. "Today we shall be introducing the poetry we will be studying. It will run from the seventeenth and eighteenth centuries to modern times. Some of you may believe that today's poetry can be found only in rap music. I intend to disabuse you of that notion."

At the mention of rap music, Marko Lane began snapping his fingers and tapping his foot. On his way to school, he had heard a rap song with a great beat, and it was coming back to him. The Blastin Caps was one of his favorite new groups.

Mr. Myers consulted his seating chart. "Marko Lane, are you snapping your fingers?" he demanded.

"Uh sorry," Marko replied with a grin. "I just heard this song from the Blastin Caps. It's going up fast in the charts. You know how it is when you get a beat going in your head."

"Mr. Lane," the teacher snarled, "do not snap your fingers and tap your feet in this class, *ever*. I could not care less what trash you like during your own personal time. In this class, we shall study serious and worthwhile poetry and prose. It offends me that so many people think this hip-hop is the only black contribution to the arts. Are those insufferable hoodlums, hip-hopping around to a beat, the best we can do? I think not."

Mr. Myers glanced around the room. "Sadly, I doubt anyone of your generation has ever heard of the great black poets of the past. For example, can anyone tell me about Claude McKay and something he wrote?"

Oliver Randall, whose father taught astronomy at the community college, raised his hand. "McKay was a major poet from the Harlem Renaissance in the 1920s. He wrote the poem 'If I Must Die,' which is probably his most famous work."

Jaris thought Oliver Randall was too smart. Oliver was one of Jaris's close friends. He was one of the guys who hung with Jaris and his other friends. They'd eat lunch every day under the eucalyptus trees in a corner of the campus. Still, he made Jaris feel like an idiot. Jaris had never heard of Claude McKay, and he had barely heard of the Harlem Renaissance. Probably nobody else in this class knew anything about it either—except for Oliver.

Oliver sat there and recited the first lines of the poem, "'If we must die, let it not be like hogs, hunted and penned in an inglorious spot.'"

Mr. Myers looked as though he had died and gone to heaven. He trembled with happy rapture. He had found a glowing gem in what he feared was a slough of mediocrity. "Thank you, Mr. Randall," he responded with joy.

At the end of class, Mr. Myers called the students' attention to a stack of literary journals on a table. His poetry had appeared in these magazines. Jaris glanced at the covers. The magazines had strange names like *Mississippi Mud Ink* and *Bayou Bard*.

Marko was standing right behind Jaris. He picked up one of the magazines and flipped through the index. He snickered and whispered to Jaris, "Look, here's his poem—'Reflections at Daybreak.' I bet that's a snoozer. What a crock." Then Marko turned to Mr. Myers and asked, "Can we borrow one of these?"

Mr. Myers looked pleased. “Certainly,” he replied.

“So, how much they pay you for a poem like this?” Marko asked.

Jaris winced. He didn’t know much about the publishing or writing business. But he did know that small literary magazines like this paid only in copies. Jaris had had a teacher in fifth grade who had several such poems published. That’s how she was paid.

“The small journals pay very little,” Mr. Myers snorted, obviously embarrassed by the question. “One publishes here for prestige, not profit.”

Marko was soon outside the classroom, laughing with Jasmine over Mr. Myer’s poem.

“Listen to this junk,” he chuckled. “It don’t even rhyme.”

> Light comes so slowly, as though afraid. . .
> Not knowing yet the perils of the day.

Jasmine giggled. “No wonder they don’t pay anything,” she remarked.

Jaris noticed Oliver coming out with his girlfriend, Alonee Lennox, just as Marko saw them.

"Hey, Randall," Marko barked, "you're a freakin' oddball. You must be crazy or somethin'. How do you know all about some old poet who died a hundred years ago or something? This McKay. I mean, who ever heard of the dude? I bet nobody else on this campus ever heard of him. And you can even recite lines from his poem? What kinda freakin' creep are you?"

Jaris hated to admit it, even to himself, but he halfway agreed with Marko. Claude McKay might have been important in his time, but what Marko said was probably true. Oliver Randall was the only student at Tubman High who had ever heard of him, much less be able quote from his poetry.

"My father was fascinated by the Harlem Renaissance," Oliver explained. "He told me all about it. Claude McKay was a giant of that era. He wrote the kind of protest poetry that just wasn't being done anywhere else."

"Old Myers looked at you like you were a wonder of nature," Jasmine complained. "You made all the resta us look like morons. We all just chopped liver with you around."

A girl from the class made a comment. "Mr. Myers wants to get his novel published. My mom and his wife play bunko. She told my mom."

Marko waved *Mississippi Mud Ink* and crowed, "He writes like a jackass. Nobody gonna want his junk."

Oliver shook his head. He and Alonee walked on. Jaris went with them. A few of the others stayed behind, laughing. Marko and Jasmine continued to ridicule Mr. Myer's poem.

As they walked away, Alonee had a sad look on her face, but Oliver looked angry. "What's with that dude?" he fumed. "I've only been at Tubman a few months, so I don't know Marko real well. Jaris, you've known him a long time. What's his problem? What's going on with this guy?"

Jaris shrugged. "He likes to make fun of people," Jaris responded. "His father is a rich businessman, walking around with gold chains. Seems like Marko needs to be hurting somebody to feel good about himself. Right Alonee? You've known him long as me."

"Yeah," Alonee agreed. "He's kind of a super creep."

"You got that right," said Sami Archer, who just caught up with them. "Jaris, that Marko givin' poor Sereeta a hard time about her mama this mornin'. I know the Good Book says we gotta love our enemies. But it's hard to love Marko. That's like lovin' the old snake who's fixin' to bite ya."

Jaris was sick to learn that Marko had already victimized Sereeta—first thing in the morning. "Some psychologists," Jaris suggested, "they say when kids are treated mean, they take it out on other people. But from what I know, Marko's never had a problem like that."

Kevin Walker, another of Jaris's friends, joined the group. Kevin had come to Tubman from Texas just last year. "Some people are just mean for no reason," he declared. "They just are. There's no accounting for it. I think sometimes they need to be stamped out like scorpions."

Jaris split from the group and walked to his next class. He kept thinking about Sereeta. She didn't need Marko's taunts on her first day as a senior. Jaris clenched and unclenched his hands in frustration. He was thinking that maybe Kevin had it right.

Chelsea Spain's first class was with Ms. Colbert, freshman science. Most of her friends were in it too. She thought it would be her favorite class. She walked in with Athena and grinned at Maurice Moore and Heston Crawford. She felt right at home. She felt as if she had been going to Tubman for a long time instead of just starting.

Best of all, there was Ms. Colbert. She was taking the roll call and setting up her first class of the school year.

This past summer, Chelsea, her friends, and Shadrach took care of the wounded and orphaned opossums at the refuge. Shadrach was known as the opossum rescue man. Ms. Colbert and Shadrach had taken the students to watch an opossum released back into the wild. So Chelsea didn't have the usual feeling she had for teachers when it came to Ms. Colbert. She looked at Ms. Colbert not so much as a teacher as a friend.

"You've all had science in middle school and elementary school," Ms. Colbert began. "Our class will deal with life science more deeply than you've seen before. We really need to deepen our knowledge of science in our country."

Chelsea leaned back and whispered to Athena Edson, who was sitting right behind her. "Yeah, a lot of other countries are way ahead of us in science. That's hurtin' us a lot. I saw a program on TV that—"

"Chelsea Spain," Ms. Colbert interrupted curtly, "are you accustomed to talking when your teachers are talking?"

Chelsea was shocked. She had no idea Ms. Colbert would scold her like that in front of everybody. They were friends! Chelsea had ridden in her van. They were colleagues at the opossum rescue refuge.

"Uh, I'm sorry, Ms. Colbert, but I—" Chelsea stammered, her face hot with embarrassment.

"There's a firm rule in this classroom," Ms. Colbert stated. "When students have something to say, they raise their hands and, when recognized, they speak. There are no exceptions to this rule. I don't know what some of you have experienced in middle school. But make no mistake. There will be no whispering or chatting with friends in classroom time."

Chelsea glimpsed her old enemy from Anderson Middle school, Kanika Brewster. She was looking right at Chelsea and grinning at her misery. Chelsea had been at

Tubman for four minutes. Already she was in trouble with someone she thought would be her favorite teacher.

Ms. Colbert was discussing the class outline, but Chelsea could barely look at her. Chelsea could not understand how the teacher could be so different. She had been nice and friendly when she was driving them to the opossum refuge. Now she had turned into a tyrant. Chelsea had not meant to be disrespectful. She just wanted to share some information with Athena.

As the students filed out of the classroom, Chelsea hurried. She did not want to make eye contact with Ms. Colbert. Not today anyway.

"You sure messed up, Spain," Kanika crowed. "She's got your number, motormouth."

"Oh shut up," Chelsea snapped. "It's no big deal."

Kanika's friend, Hana, pointed to Chelsea and asked, "How come you're wearing those baggy clothes?"

Kanika and Hana laughed as they walked away.

Athena was now beside Chelsea. "Don't sweat it, Chelsea. Ms. Colbert will forget all about it tomorrow."

"No, she won't," Chelsea groaned privately to Athena. "I made a bad impression *the first day*. That'll stick with her."

"Don't be silly," Athena insisted.

"Athena," Chelsea cried, "everything is wrong! I acted like a fool, and I look like a freak! I could just die!"

# CHAPTER TWO

When lunchtime came, the group Chelsea belonged to had pledged to meet beneath two pepper trees. The trees had very distinctive gnarled branches, and they stood in the west corner of the freshman eating area. They knew of a nice spot there with plenty of room for Chelsea, Athena, Keisha, Inessa, Falisha, and Maurice and Heston. Chelsea was pretty sure they would not all show up. They weren't a tight group like Jaris's group—Alonee's posse. Besides, nothing was turning out right for Chelsea on this terrible day. She needed the support of her friends, but the only one she was sure of was Athena. No doubt, everybody else was having a wonderful, exciting day. They had probably all made new friends. They wouldn't want to meet Chelsea and her lame group under the pepper trees.

Chelsea didn't want to further demolish her self-esteem by being the first one to show up. She would at least wait for Athena so that they could go together. Chelsea didn't want to feel like a bigger fool than she already did. And she would feel like that if she was sitting there by herself when Athena showed up. Athena would think, "What a loser! How did I get stuck with *her*?"

But, as Chelsea looked over at the pepper trees, she saw Falisha and Keisha already there. They were just opening their brown lunch bags. Chelsea's spirits rose. She skipped down the little path and sang out, "Hi, guys!"

Keisha looked up and replied, "Hey, I'm glad *somebody*'s having a good day and feels all cheery. I'm in the dumps, girl."

"*Nobody*'s having the kind of day I'm having," Falisha announced. "I even dropped the little plastic pudding container. Look, it spattered all over my white blouse!"

Chelsea's spirits rose still higher. She was not alone in her misery after all. She sat down quickly and pulled an orange from her bag. "This isn't even a good orange," she remarked. "It's fulla seeds! Oh, but the worst is that I'm already in trouble in science. Ms. Colbert yelled at me as if I was some criminal just 'cause I whispered something real fast to Athena."

"You think Colbert is bad?" Keisha groaned. "I got Lyman for science. He looks like a lizard. He's got these beady little eyes that can look left and right at the same time, I swear. He watches us like a hawk. He has this little raspy voice, and I can't understand a word he's saying. I asked a perfectly nice question. He goes 'If you can't even understand a simple thing like erosion, then maybe you should go back to middle school.'"

"Yeah," Falisha added. "He was talking about rocks or something. So I asked him if that was gonna be on the test. And he like went crazy, didn't he, Keisha? He goes, 'Don't you *ever* ask me if something is gonna be on the next test!' "

Athena appeared then, followed by Heston. Inessa and Maurice brought up the rear. Chelsea looked at them all in amazement. Everybody came!

"Nobody's talkin' to me," Heston complained. "Everybody hates me. I start talkin' to somebody, and they walk away. Nobody has *ever* liked me. Mom says that's not true, but she's a mom."

"We like you, Heston," Chelsea consoled. "I *really* like you."

"It's like you're too shy, dude," Maurice pointed out. "You like say 'Hi' in a squeaky little voice. You're kinda like hopin' nobody answers you. Then you're hurt when they don't."

"I never know what to talk about," Heston declared.

Maurice grinned. "Here's the deal, man. I'm gonna tell you my secret now, so lissen up. This works with everybody, but especially with chicks. Chicks, they wanna be talkin' all the time. You smile and listen, right? They love that. They think you're interested in what they're sayin' even though you're bored stiff. Keep smilin' and nodding. Once in a while go 'right' or 'yeah!' You could care less about anything she's been rattling on about. But she's gonna think you're great. Chicks love to yak."

Chelsea laughed. "You got it all figured out, huh, Maurice?"

"'Nother thing," Maurice went on, still grinning, "if you're good at anything, help somebody with their homework. They'll love you for that. You're good in science, Heston. That should help you there."

Heston chomped on his sandwich and reflected on what Maurice had said.

In a few moments, Falisha spoke. "You know what, you guys? My mom won't let me be alone in the house when she goes out. She makes my grandma come and sit with me like I'm a baby. I'm old enough to babysit myself, and I gotta be watched! Mom tells me she needs a 'night out with the girls,' but that's a big lie. Mom has a boyfriend, that creepy guy Shadrach who takes care of hurt opossums. Mom knows how I feel about him. So when she's goin' out with him, she makes up lies. But I'm not stupid."

"Shadrach's a pretty nice guy, Falisha," Athena commented. "Me and Chelsea and the guys help out at the opossum refuge. We're even feeding the babies now."

"You gotta be real careful threading the feeding tube down the baby opossum's neck. Shadrach was so patient in teaching us," Chelsea added.

Inessa spoke up. "I don't blame you for freakin' about that guy, Falisha. He's scary-looking."

"I wish Mom wouldn't date anybody," Falisha admitted. "I mean, me and Mom get along good together. I don't know why things can't just stay that way. We don't need a guy in the house. We go places and we watch TV together and eat popcorn. We have a lot of fun. I love being with my mom. She's like a big sister. I don't know why she even wants to spoil everything and get a boyfriend."

Falisha looked down sadly at her sandwich, pulling out a strip of ham. "It wouldn't be *our* house anymore with a stranger there."

Jaris went to the first meeting of the Advanced Placement American History class with Ms. McDowell. She looked at the ten students and smiled. "I think this will be an excellent class. I know all of you from my junior history classes. You're all up to the work in this class if you put in a good effort."

Oliver Randall and Alonee Lennox were there, along with Sereeta Prince and Marko Lane. Kevin Walker might have been able to handle it too. But he wanted to put more time in on his track and boxing practice. Both he and Trevor Jenkins had high hopes for the Tubman track team this year.

The reading list was very big, and a lot of research would be required. Ms. McDowell reminded everyone how fortunate they were. They could access original sources in libraries all over America by going online.

Compared to Oliver, Alonee, and Sereeta, Jaris felt he was the dumbest. Oliver and Alonee were very bright, and Sereeta was smarter than Jaris. Jaris always had to struggle for the top grades that he usually earned. He had always been an overachiever, grasping at his high goals by his fingertips. He was driven by years of hearing Pop complain about his own missed chances in life. Jaris wanted to do the best he could or even better. Jaris wanted to be a teacher—an outstanding teacher like Ms. McDowell or Mom. Maybe, he thought, he would like to teach college and write too.

Jaris smiled, chuckling to himself as he scanned the reading list. It was daunting. The research was going to be tough to manage. And then the critical test came at the end of the course to determine whether you were worthy of credit for college.

Jaris knew he was overreaching. He chuckled again. Pop had once told him, "If you don't reach for the stars, boy, you won't even make it to the top of the barn."

At the end of the day, Jaris waited for Chelsea so that he could drive her home. Once again, he lamented her stupid error in judgment that got her grounded and made him her personal driver. If Chelsea could go home by herself, Jaris wouldn't have to wait forever while she chatted with her many friends.

"Come on, chili pepper," Jaris muttered to himself. He had to get home to start his homework for AP American History. Then he wanted to catch up with Trevor at the Chicken Shack, where they both earned extra money.

Finally, Chelsea came. "Hi, Jare! How's being a senior?"

"Lotta work, chili pepper," Jaris answered. "How'd your day go?"

"Oh, ups and downs," she reported. "I got in trouble with my science teacher for whispering in class. I thought Ms. Colbert was my friend, but she's a regular meanie."

"Well, the way kids jabber away in some of these classes," Jaris explained, "you can barely hear the teacher. I remember sitting through those English classes with Mr. Pippin and ending up with nothing. The creeps like Marko drowned him out. Ms. Colbert was probably right to crack down first day, even if it was on you."

"I guess," Chelsea agreed. "But I just whispered something real fast to Athena."

"Thirty-three kids all whispering at once," Jaris insisted, "that can drown out a teacher real fast. Jaris edged his Honda into the stream of cars leaving Tubman.

"Yeah," Chelsea objected, "but I liked her so much. I looked at her like my friend. We all worked at the opossum rescue place. She drove us there and stuff. I thought she liked me too. Now she's mad at me, and she probably hates me for talking in class the first day."

"She doesn't hate you, chili pepper," Jaris told his sister. "Nobody could hate you. Ms. Colbert just wanted to get off on the right foot. She used you as an example to scare everybody else. She needed the kids to know from the gitgo that she can't be pushed around. That's the mistake poor Mr. Pippin made. He was weak. Marko and those clowns got the best of him, and it never stopped. Mr. Pippin is actually a good teacher, but the chaos in that room made learning impossible."

Chelsea chewed on that idea for a while. Then she remembered something she wanted to tell her brother.

"Jaris," she began, "I called Maya Archer last night. She told me everybody's making fun of poor Sereeta's mom. Jare, can't Sereeta's mom go to rehab or something? I saw on TV where some famous people had problems with drinking, and they got helped at a rehab place."

"Yeah, it would be great if she did that, Chelsea," Jaris agreed. "But first she has to admit she's got a problem. She denies it all the time. Nobody can force you to get help unless you break the law and get sentenced to rehab or something. Otherwise, you have to make up your own mind. You have to go to rehab because *you* want to go."

Jaris drove quietly for a few seconds. "Sereeta loves her mom so much," he finally said. "I'm scared her mom'll get in an accident and be hurt or killed. If that happened, I'm not sure Sereeta could come back from that."

Later, Jaris went over to the Chicken Shack. He wasn't working tonight, but he wanted to speak with his friend, Trevor. Trevor was working more hours at the Chicken Shack these days. Things were better for him at home now. His mother, Mickey Jenkins, had eased up on her tough discipline and allowed him some freedom. She finally admitted that he was a good kid and that he didn't need her yelling in his face all the time.

Mickey Jenkins was raising her four boys by herself after alcohol drove her husband into the gutter. She slaved long hours in a nursing home to raise her boys. The oldest two were now in the United States Army. The third was in the community college, and Trevor was a senior at Tubman. He was the baby, and his ma was finally ready to give him some room to fly.

"I didn't see you at lunch, Trev," Jaris remarked. He was talking to Trevor from the other side of the counter. "How was your first day as a senior?"

"Great," Trevor replied with a grin. "When I'm done working here, I got a date!"

"Way to go, dude," Jaris responded. Jaris really liked Trevor. He was one of the good guys. Trevor didn't have a lot of luck with chicks. His ma had made it hard for him to date until recently. Trevor's first real girlfriend was a beautiful sixteen-year-old who dyed her hair red—Vanessa Allen. She had dropped out of Tubman in her sophomore year and left home. She had moved in with an older sister and the sister's wild boyfriend, Bo.

Trevor's mother hated Vanessa. She had no use for any high school dropout, much less for a girl who left home at such an early age. But Trevor finally won his mother over and started dating Vanessa. Disaster was the result. Vanessa duped Trevor into driving a getaway car for Bo when he stole things from a drugstore. Trevor knew he could have gotten into real trouble. He finally wised up and dumped Vanessa. Since then, he had been having a dismal social life. Jaris felt sorry for him when everybody else was planning fun weekends with their girlfriends.

"So who's the chick, Trevor? She go to Tubman?" Jaris asked.

Trevor paused as he made a chicken sandwich. Trevor was great at fixing food and working at the counter. He was an excellent employee, and he was always getting raises. Trevor was piling on the chicken and a slice of American cheese. Then came the pickles, tomatoes, and lettuce. He added a final dash of the store's Super Sauce.

Trevor was Jaris's closest friend. There was nothing the two boys wouldn't do for each other. Trevor was the closest to being a brother that Jaris had. But now Trevor seemed secretive, unwilling to share. "Uh, she doesn't go to Tubman right now," Trevor answered evasively. "She's uh . . . not in school right now."

"What's goin' on, man?" Jaris asked. "What's the big secret about this chick?"

Trevor wrapped the sandwich, with the folded paper napkin sticking out of the top fold.

"Uh . . . well, lissen man," Trevor said. "You're my bro. I know that whatever you say to me, you got my best interests at heart. I mean, your mom went to bat for me with my ma, and got Ma off my case. She finally stopped tryin' to control my life twenty-four-seven, and I owe you and your ma for that."

Jaris had a sinking feeling. Trevor wouldn't be beating around the bush if the chick wasn't bad news. Jaris took a shot in the dark, and he was afraid he was going to be right. "Man, you're not with Vanessa Allen again, are you, Trev?" Jaris asked.

Trevor scooped a portion of french fries into a bag and put it next to the sandwich.

All the while working, he took a deep breath and finally answered. "Jaris, lissen. People change. They do. Vanessa's seventeen now. She don't work at the Ice House anymore. You know that. She took some classes at one of those career colleges, and she's workin' at a spa doing massages. She's makin' good money, and she's like a whole different person, man."

"Dude," Jaris reminded him, "think about when you drove that car for Bo. She knew what was going down. You thought you were taking him to the drugstore to get cough medicine. Vanessa knew all along what was goin' down. They wanted you sitting at the wheel of the car while he came running out with stolen property. Trevor, what if the drugstore manager had caught him and fought—if he'd been hurt or killed? You woulda got busted along with him, maybe for murder. Vanessa would let that happen to you, dude."

"I know, Jaris," Trevor admitted. "I know all that, but that was last year. Vanessa doesn't have anythin' to do with her sister and Bo anymore. Vanessa told me a hundred times how sorry she was that I was put in that spot. Vanessa's sister and Bo moved to Las Vegas. She doesn't even have their address. She's cut off from them, and she wants it like that."

The customer had paid for the food and was approaching the pickup counter.

"Vanessa and another girl got a little apartment over near the spa where she works," Trevor went on. "She's workin' on her GED too, Jaris. She's hittin' the books. She really wants to live a good life now. She wants me to be a part of it, 'cause she cares for me. Jaris, please, don't be against me on this. Your support, man, it means the world to me."

Trevor bagged the sandwich, fries, and soda. He tossed extra ketchup packets in and put the bag on top of the counter. He smiled at the customer and said cheerily, "Thank you. Come again!"

The Trevor turned to Jaris and spoke. "Trust me on this, Jaris. I love the girl. I loved her from the start. I dumped her when she lied to me about cuttin' off with Bo and her sister. But now she don't lie anymore. She's up front. She's really tryin' to turn it all around, man." Trevor's voice was filled with emotion.

"Okay, Trev," Jaris relented. "If this is what you think is right, I'm not gonna argue with you. I'm just asking you to do one thing, man. Keep your eyes wide open. If something looks fishy, don't make excuses for her. Just get out of there, man. The time for excuses is over. If it's not one hundred percent on the up and up, *run*. Y'hear what I'm saying?"

Trevor nodded. "That's fair. I hear ya, man. I'm no fool. Thanks, bro." He reached out and clasped the other boy's hand. Then they hugged briefly.

As they worked, Jaris took the lulls in business at the Chicken Shack to share his own misgivings about taking the AP American History class.

"Most of the other seniors in there," Jaris declared, "they're way smarter than me, Trevor. Oliver is a freakin' genius, and Alonee isn't far behind. Sereeta is so bright too. I'm swimming as fast as I can, but I feel like I'm in way over my head. Still, I need to do this. I want to test myself to see what I got. It's like those guys who drag themselves up Mount Everest, I guess. Even if you think you're not gonna make it, you gotta try."

"I hear ya," Trevor responded. "Like you told Sereeta once, you gotta take risks. You can't always play it safe."

Between customers, Jaris and Trevor chatted a little while about their first day as seniors. Then Jaris left the store.

# CHAPTER THREE

Jaris drove past the Manley house just to reassure himself that everything looked okay. He looked at the lovely two-story home. The lawn was perfectly manicured. The shrubs along the driveway were pruned just right. And a beautiful stone stag stood in the front yard.

Jaris chuckled. That was just what Shadrach had joked about. Most rich folks didn't want to mess so much with real wildlife. But they didn't mind stone statues of animals in their yards.

Jaris thought his conversation with Chelsea. Would Mrs. Manley go into rehab for her alcohol problem? If only—he thought—if only she would.

Jaris slowed the car down as he passed by. He noticed that Perry Manley's Jaguar was not in its usual place in the driveway. Sereeta's stepfather always parked his car in the driveway except overnight, when he put his car in the garage. But Olivia Manley's car was in the driveway.

On an impulse, Jaris pulled into the driveway. Maybe, he thought, this would be a good time to talk to Sereeta's mother. Jaris hadn't had much opportunity to talk to her one on one, just the two of them. Maybe this was his opportunity. Maybe Jaris could explain things gently to Olivia Manley. He might make her see that the stories of her drinking bouts were fodder for neighborhood gossip. They were all over Tubman High now too, hurting Sereeta. Surely Mrs. Manley wouldn't want her daughter to be hurt and embarrassed any more.

Jaris rang the doorbell. He was expecting a maid or a nanny to come to the door. But Sereeta's mother was standing there in a beautiful red silk lounging outfit. She was not drunk, but she was buzzed. She had a glass of wine in her hand. The evening was young, and Jaris figured it would only get worse.

"Oh hello," Olivia Manley greeted. She paused, trying to remember the boy's name. "Jaris. Jaris Spain, right?" she asked in a little girl's voice. She always had a light, fragile voice. When she was drinking, her tone became childish, tinged with vulnerability. "You're looking for Sereeta? She doesn't live here anymore. I thought you knew."

"May I come in for a minute, Mrs. Manley?" Jaris asked. "I wanted to talk to you if that's all right."

"Come in," the woman replied, stepping back.

Jaris stepped into the front room. It was beautifully furnished. The Spain house had nice, comfy furniture. But nothing in Jaris's home would rate a spread in the Sunday *Homes and Gardens* feature.

He was very nervous. He began to think it was a horrible idea even to come here in the first place. Jaris was only seventeen, going on eighteen. How could he think for a moment that he could persuade this woman to do anything? How dare he come to lecture somebody old enough to be his mother?

Jaris sat down on one of the leather chairs, and Mrs. Manley seated herself opposite him, on the sofa. She refilled her wine glass from a bottle on the coffee table.

"Mrs. Manley," Jaris began. "Sereeta doesn't know I've come here. She would have probably told me not to come. She's very worried about you."

"Oh my goodness!" Olivia Manley exclaimed, taking a long drink from her wine glass. "That dear child. Why in the world is she worried about me? I'm perfectly fine."

"Mrs. Manley, I know you're an educated woman," Jaris went on.

"Thank you very much," she interrupted him. "Not many people understand that. My husband Perry, for one, thinks I'm ignorant because I don't have a job. But

I've had two years of college and I did very well. I was on the dean's list, I'll have you know." Her voice began to take on the petulant qualities of onrushing drunkenness.

Jaris was now convinced he should get up and leave. But he couldn't think of a way to do that without looking stupid. Instead, he just started blabbing what was on his mind.

"You know about addictions and how terrible they can be, Mrs. Manley," Jaris continued. "They happen to all kinds of people—smart, talented people. They're like any other sickness. When somebody is addicted to drugs or alcohol, you know, they need help, professional help. You know, you can't do it yourself—"

"What are you talking about, young man?" Mrs. Manley demanded, an edge to her voice.

Part of Jaris felt like running out the door. But he couldn't help himself. He just kept digging himself into a deeper hole.

"Mrs. Manley, I'm sorry to say this, but I think you have a problem with alcohol,"

Jaris blurted. "If you went to a rehab center, they could help you get well again. That would mean so much to Sereeta, to have her mom healthy again."

There, he had said what was on his mind. Mrs. Manley stood up. She was not steady on her feet, but she wasn't about to collapse either. She steadied herself by holding onto the back of a chair next to the sofa with her left hand. Her right hand held the wine glass.

"How dare you?" she cried. "How dare you come here and insinuate that I am a drunkard? I am so insulted I cannot bear it. I never drink more than a glass of wine, one harmless little glass of wine!"

"Mrs. Manley, please forgive me," Jaris persisted. "It's just that you *do* have a problem. You need help, and I was hoping I could convince you to—"

"I must say, Jaris Spain," Olivia Manley declared, "you are a very rude and unpleasant young man. I shall tell my daughter how you came here and found me drinking a small glass of wine. She'll know how you used that against me to imply that I am some drunkard. This is an outrage."

"Mrs. Manley," Jaris went on desperately, against all odds, "the other night you were downtown at that bar. Sereeta and I had to bring you home, and you had trouble walking. You were drinking at the Green Hornet Café and causing a disturbance. They were going to call the police. We brought you home here, and the neighbors saw how . . . uh . . . wobbly you were. Now they're gossiping, and it hurts Sereeta so much. She loves you, and she just wants you to be well."

The situation was now way out of control. He had rung the doorbell on an impulse. He should have thought about what he was doing. He realized he had made a *big* mistake.

"That is a lie!" Mrs. Manley declared. "That is a terrible lie. I never heard of that place. The Green Hornet Café indeed! I have never been to such a place in my life. I cannot believe you would come here and lie like this. What a terrible young man you are to tell such dreadful lies!"

The woman drained her wine glass and put it down. "How can you do this to me?" she demanded. "Did Perry put you up to this? I think he's trying to drive me insane. Yes, he'll stop at nothing. And you . . . you're in league with him. It's all very clear to me now."

"Is Mr. Manley coming home soon?" Jaris asked.

"Yes!" Mrs. Manley replied, almost shouting. "And I will tell him just what I think of this ugly little drama. Now get out of my house before I call the police, Jaris Spain."

Jaris's heart was pounding. His mind was a jumble of regrets and feelings. He couldn't think straight. "What have I done?" was his only real thought.

Jaris went out the door and to his car. Before he got into his Honda, Mr. Manley's Jaguar pulled into the driveway. Within seconds, Jaris and Mr. Manley were staring at each other.

"Mr. Manley, I'm Jaris Spain, Sereeta's friend and—" Jaris began to say.

"I know who you are. What do you want?" the man snapped.

Despite the man's abrupt reply, Jaris thought he had a second chance. Maybe he could get Mr. Manley to help him.

"Mr. Manley," Jaris explained, "Sereeta is so worried about her mother. Is there any chance of getting her into rehab? She's out of control. Something needs to be done."

"Something is going to be done," Mr. Manley replied bitterly. "I'm going to file for divorce."

"But," Jaris gasped, "what will happen to her?"

"That's none of your business," Mr. Manley answered curtly. "Tonight, her sister and brother-in-law are coming from San Francisco. I expect them around nine."

Jaris noticed then that the man was shaking. His wife's condition apparently was taking its toll on him.

"I'm sorry, Mr. Manley. I really am," Jaris said sincerely.

Perry Manley nodded and hurried in the house.

Jaris got into his car and left the Manley house. About a block away, he pulled over to the curb. He needed to call his mother on his cell phone. "Mom, I'll be late coming home tonight. Sereeta's mother is drinking a lot again. Mrs. Manley's sister and her brother-in-law are coming down to be with her. I think maybe they'll see about rehab for her or something. I'm going over to tell Sereeta and see if I can help her in any way."

"Okay, sweetie," Mom replied. "If there's anything we can do, just let us know. When Livy and I were close, we would go shopping with Gayla, her sister. She's very nice. Gayla is very steady, a kind of earth-mother type."

"Thanks, Mom," Jaris said.

He drove directly over to Sereeta's house. Sereeta answered his knock on the door. She took one look at Jaris and asked in a frightened voice, "Is something wrong?"

"Well, no, but we need to talk," Jaris responded.

"Let's sit on the bench under the trees," Sereeta suggested. "Grandma's taking a nap in the house."

When they were seated, Sereeta spoke. "What's the matter, Jaris? It's something with my mother, isn't it?"

"Yeah, Sereeta," he replied. Jaris's head was down. He couldn't look at Sereeta. "I went over there on an impulse to try to talk to her, and it didn't work out so good. Chelsea said something about maybe your mom could go into rehab. Well, I was stupid enough to suggest that to her, and she got real defensive. Babe, I really booted it. I don't know what made me do it. Your mom hates me, and Mr. Manley wasn't so friendly either."

"Oh Jare!" Sereeta sighed. "You can be impulsive. Most of the time, that makes you very dear to me. Sometimes . . ."

Jaris nodded his head in agreement. "I know. I know," he said.

Then Jaris turned and looked squarely at his girl. "Your mom," he told her, "she was drinking and stuff. Then Perry came home, and he was all shaky and angry. Sereeta, he said he's filing for divorce."

"Oh Lord!" Sereeta cried. Jaris put his arms around her and held her tightly.

"Baby, it's not all bad," he consoled her. "Your mom's sister and her husband are coming down from San Francisco tonight. They're gonna try to work something out."

A tiny glimmer of hope flashed in Sereeta's eyes. "Oh, Aunt Gayla is such a good person. She's strong too. She's about ten years older than Mom. She's always been able to get through to Mom when nobody else could."

"Then they'll probably get your mom into rehab, Sereeta," Jaris assured her. "That would make all the difference. She needs something like that. She needs professional help. I don't know if Perry meant that stuff about a divorce but—"

"They've been fighting almost every day," Sereeta cut in. "It's become a regular show for the neighbors. And it's all over school, thanks to people like Marko. Marko thinks it's funny to talk about how people walk and talk when they're drunk. I remember when I was little. There was a man, he'd stagger home from the bar each night. The boys would walk after him, imitating him. They'd say he was 'measuring the sidewalk.' I remember them saying that and laughing."

"I'm sorry, babe," Jaris responded.

"Kevin Walker's in my science class," Sereeta commented. "He told me today he'd like to waylay Marko and beat him to within an inch of his life. I told Kevin not even to think of doing that. But in my heart, Jaris, I do hate Marko. I mean, I never wanted to hate anybody. It's such a terrible thing—hate. It like destroys the person who's doing that hating, and I know that. I never wanted to feel like that. But if I heard that something bad happened to Marko, I'd be happy. I'd be ashamed of being happy, but I couldn't stop the feeling."

"Babe," Jaris told her, "I think things will change now for the better. I really do."

"Thanks for coming over and telling me, Jaris," Sereeta said to her boyfriend. "Later on, I'll call the house and talk to Aunt Gayla. She and I always got along. We text each other once a month at least. She never forgets my birthday. I feel so much better knowing that she's gonna be there."

Jaris leaned over and kissed Sereeta. "I love you, babe," he said softly.

"Love you back," Sereeta whispered.

When Jaris got home, Mom and Pop were talking in the living room, coffee cups in hand. Pop looked up and asked, "They finally getting some help for that poor lady? I remember in the old days when Olivia's sister lived down here. Gayla and Artie

Chandler were good people. Artie and I played pool. He's a regular guy. Then they moved to the Bay Area. Was a bad thing for Olivia, you know. Gayla was a rock in her life. Life's a rough business. We need all the rocks we can find."

"You know," Jaris responded, "Sereeta has been going through so much pain with people talking about her mother. That jerk Marko Lane's been joking about it at school. Today, he was yelling at Sereeta and asking if her mom is still drinking."

"That creep!" Pop fumed. "Old Jackson was tellin' me 'bout Marko's father, the dude with the gold chains around his neck. He just bought the social club across the street from the apartments on Grant Avenue. He's gonna rent it out for weddings, stuff like that."

Pop took a sip of coffee. "Jackson, he's comin' 'round the shop these days. That's a different man now. He's just got so bored after he sold the fixit shop to me. He's good company on a long working day. Gotta admit, he's got some good tips too."

Pop put his coffee cup down. "Any-ways," he continued, "Jackson, he said some old dude who's kinda soft in the head sold Lane the building for like nothin'. Lane took the old guy for a ride. The old man didn't realize what the place was worth. Lane just got his slimy lawyers to fast-talk him into a rotten deal. They convinced the old guy that the building was a piece of trash—he'd be lucky to unload it at any price. Now the old guy's son is freakin' out 'cause the property was gonna be his inheritance. That's how Lane has gotten so rich—swindling people."

Pop glanced over at Mom, who said nothing. Pop went on. "Lane, he brought Marko up without any principles, and now the boy's the creep he is. All that matters is having gold chains around your neck and strutting around like The Man."

Mom shook her head and added what she knew. "I've talked to Marko's mother a few times. She runs that house-cleaning business. At first, she did all the work herself, but now she has a big crew. She's making money hand over fist. She doesn't have much to do with her husband. Marko lives with her, but he's his father's son. He idolizes his father."

"Two peas in a pod, Jerk Sr. and Jerk Jr.," Pop sneered with disgust.

Just before ten that night, Jaris was working at his computer. Sereeta called and sounded upbeat.

"Jaris," she reported, "I talked to Aunt Gayla. She said Mom is resting now. Tomorrow they're going to drive to this really nice rehab place, about twenty-five miles from here. They're taking her around four in the afternoon. Aunt Gayla is picking me up, and I can ride with them and be with my mom, you know. I can go with her to her room, and help her . . . get . . ." Sereeta started sobbing, but she tried to control it. "I can help her, you know, settle in and like that."

"That's great, babe," Jaris told her. "I think this is gonna be the beginning of something good."

"Yeah," Sereeta agreed. "Aunt Gayla says Mom is kinda scared, but she knows she's in trouble. When the alcohol wears off, she knows. She comes out of these binges, and she's shaky and sick. Then she knows she's in trouble. When we were in San Francisco that time, Mom came right out and told me how awful the hangovers were. She said how she didn't remember anything but being so sick she wanted to die."

Before she hung up, Sereeta said, "I finally have a little hope, Jaris. I finally do."

As Jaris closed the phone, Chelsea appeared in the doorway. "Sereeta?" she asked.

"Yeah, chili pepper," Jaris nodded. "Looks like her mom's going to get the help she needs—finally. Her sister's come down from Frisco. They're taking her to a rehab center tomorrow. Sereeta's going with them to help her mom settle in."

"I'm glad!" Chelsea exclaimed. "Did I ever tell you about the time Mom and Sereeta's mom were shoppin' together and I was with them? I got my chocolate ice cream all over my cute new pink dress. Mom, she's always so calm, but this time she got all upset."

Chelsea flashed a big smile and went on. "Well, Sereeta's mom was really nice. She smiled at me and helped me get the chocolate ice cream off my dress. She called me 'princess,' and she really made me feel better. Nobody ever called me 'princess' before that. I sorta liked her a lot after that. I felt bad when people were sayin' mean things about her and hurtin' Sereeta. I'm glad she's gonna get some help now."

Jaris smiled at his little sister. "Chili pepper, you never told me that story before," he told her. "That's sweet. Thanks for telling me now. Sometime I'll tell Sereeta, and that'll make her smile."

Jaris turned back to his computer but then swung back again to face his sister.

"Hey!" he called, stopping her in the doorway. She turned to look at him. "That was a good tip," he said to his little sister. "I mean, about going to a rehab place. Thanks, chili pepper."

At school the next day, Marko Lane caught up to Trevor Jenkins as Vanessa was dropping Trevor off at school.

"Hey dude," Marko called out, "you hanging out with that dropout chick again?"

"She's working on her GED," Trevor told Marko. "And she has a great job. She's doing just fine now."

"You're a loser, Jenkins," Marko crowed. He was always angry at Trevor for beating him in the last race of last year's track season. Mr. Lane had come to see his son win. When Trevor took the race, he humiliated Marko in front of his father. "You're one big loser, and so's Vanessa Allen. Just wait until the track meets start this year. I'll leave you in my dust, dude. You winning that last race was a fluke."

Trevor stopped dead in his tracks and stood for a moment. Rage boiled in him. Marko took a step or two past him, turned, and looked at him. Perhaps he saw something in Trevor's eyes. Marko sprinted away.

Trevor needed to cool down. He already had told his mother he was seeing Vanessa again. Ma said she would trust him to do the right thing. But right now Trevor felt like smacking Marko hard, really hard. He wanted to see his teeth sprinkled across the Tubman parking lot blacktop.

Everybody else on the Tubman track team was a good sport. Trevor got along fine with Kevin Walker, Matson Malloy, and the others. Marko spoiled the team spirit for everybody. When the other guys lost, they high-fived the winner. It was competition among friends, and it was fun. Marko made it ugly. Marko wasn't in it for the good of Tubman High School. He was there for one reason: He wanted the personal glory of winning for Marko Lane.

# CHAPTER THREE

Trevor was still standing there, fuming, when Jaris happened by.

"Hey bro!" Jaris hailed. "You look like you got something dark on your mind. Wassup?"

"Ah, man!" Trevor answered. "Lane was just talkin' trash about Vanessa. You know how actors at a play tell the others to 'break a leg' for good luck? Well, I wish Marko would bust his head—and not for good luck. I wish we'd never have to see him again around this school or anywhere."

"Coach Curry has got to keep him, dude, 'cause he's one of the best runners," Jaris responded. "Don't let him make you crazy, man."

"Yeah," Trevor agreed.

"How's it goin', man?" Jaris asked.

"Me and Vanessa went to the movies," Trevor replied. "We had a good time. We saw this off-the-hook comedy, and we both laughed our heads off. She's changed a lot, Jaris. She's talking about maybe training to be a physical therapist. She thinks she wants to help people recovering from injuries. She likes this massage business 'cause she said she makes people feel better, and that's a big rush. Now she's thinking about really getting into the health field."

"That's good," Jaris affirmed. Deep in his heart, though, he was still very leery of the girl. She had lied before. She had tricked Trevor into a really dangerous situation. Jaris found it hard to forget all that.

"Desmond's coming home on leave from the army, Jaris," Trevor went on. "Me and Tommy and Desmond gonna take Ma out to a fancy dinner, like we did before. Tommy's bringing his girlfriend, and Des is bringing his chick. So Mom says it's okay if I bring Vanessa. I'm real excited about that, bro."

"Yeah," Jaris replied, smiling at his friend. "That'll be cool." Jaris clapped his best friend on the shoulder. Trevor looked so happy when he talked about Vanessa. As Trevor moved on to this first class, Jaris looked after him. Jaris hoped for the best for Trev and Vanessa. His friend deserved a break.

Jaris's thoughts turned to Sereeta and what she faced this afternoon. She was to join her aunt and uncle taking Olivia Manley to the rehab center. Would Mrs. Manley really go? Would Sereeta's mother call it off at the last minute?

Even if her mom went, the afternoon was going to be very emotional. Sereeta would probably be crying, and so would her mother. But Gayle Chandler would hold it all together. Mom had told Jaris about Mrs. Chandler. She had a big, warm laugh that made everybody feel better. She could convince almost anybody of anything with her warm good humor. If anybody could make it happen, she could.

# CHAPTER FOUR

After lunch that day, Jaris headed for English with Mr. Myers. Mr. Myers introduced the class to some of his favorite poetry from the nineteenth century. "Wordsworth," he announced, "in 'The World Is Too Much with Us,' skillfully uses vocabulary."

Marko Lane raised his hand. "Mr. Myers, I know this isn't what we are talking about, but I just wanted to tell you. I read your poem, 'Reflections on Daybreak,' and it was good. Sort of like Wordsworth." Marko was obviously trying to ingratiate himself to the teacher, but Mr. Myers did not looked pleased. He looked angry.

"'Reflections *on* Daybreak,' Mr. Lane?" Mr. Myers asked in a sarcastic voice. "That isn't the title of my poem. It is 'Reflections *at* Daybreak.'"

"Uh, yeah!" Marko sputtered. "Well it's about the same thing, huh?"

Alonee Lennox covered her mouth to keep from laughing.

"On the contrary, Mr. Lane," Mr. Myers explained. "Reflections *at* daybreak describe our thoughts as the new day dawns. Reflections *on* daybreak are thoughts about the actual physical events accompanying daybreak. They are totally different things. And, since you enjoyed my poem so much, could you describe the theme?" Mr. Myers' voice was hostile.

Marko Lane actually hated poetry, and he thought this particular poem was stupid. He had glanced at it and mocked it. He vaguely remembered something in the poem about death, so he seized on that. "I think the theme was something about death.

Like maybe the new day dawns and the old day dies or something."

"Mr. Lane," Mr. Myers intoned, "I do not appreciate sycophancy. In case you do not know the meaning of that word, which I doubt that you do, it means servile flattery. It is dishonest praise in a pathetic effort to win the approval of someone."

The teacher raised his head to address the class as a whole. "I am fully aware," he continued, "that the vast majority of you in this class have no use whatsoever for nineteenth-century poetry. You probably have no need of *any* poetry, for that matter. But I would appreciate the courtesy of honest comments, not despicable fawning. Poetry has unique value. It has a significance that is deeper than most writing. I am hoping that at least some of you experience a deeper understanding of the world. In our tests, I will ascertain that."

After class, Marko was talking with Jasmine and the little group of students who gathered. "What a pompous old grouch

Myers is," Marko fumed. "At least with Pippin we had a few laughs. This guy is about as much fun as a case of poison ivy."

"He's a frustrated writer," Jasmine offered. "I heard he's written lots of stories and novels and stuff. But the editors keep sending them back 'cause they're no good. That's why he's bitter."

"You tried to butter him up, man!" Eric Carney hooted. "And it went over like a lead balloon. You're such a phony."

Marko glared at Eric. "Hey dude, what's wrong with your face? You got some horrible contagious disease or something? Stay away from the rest of us," Marko taunted.

"It's acne, stupid," Eric replied. "Someday I'll lose the acne. But you'll still be an idiot."

Oliver Randall had helped Eric in the past when he needed tutoring. Now he drew near to him. "Man, don't waste your time messing with Marko," Oliver said in a low tone. "Just ignore him. He thinks he's a rock star or something."

Marko heard Oliver's comment and he sneered, "Know what, Randall? My father, he owns a lot of real estate around here. He bought the social hall on Grant. Pretty soon he's gonna be buying some mini malls. He's gonna own half the neighborhood. When my father walks down the street, they know he's the King. He's better than a rock star, and I'm real proud of him."

"Maybe so," Eric responded, "but you're still an idiot. You always will be."

Destini Fletcher was in the group, watching the argument. She had once dated a friend of Marko's and went to a party Marko's father hosted. Now she turned to Alonee.

"You shoulda seen Marko's father at this ritzy party Tyron Becker took me to," she remarked. "It was mega spooky. It was wild. All those fancy cars. And here's Marko's father in an Italian silk suit, I guess. So many pretty women. I even recognized some of them from TV. Wow, it was like nothing I've ever seen, but it was weird too. It was fake. I didn't like being there. I was so glad to get out in the fresh air that night."

Marko overheard what Destini was saying.

"Maybe it was too rich for your blood, girl," Marko sneered. "You live in a run-down shack at the edge of town. Your mama cleans up messes at the hospital. You don't understand first-class people like my father. You're from the slums, girl, and you got a slum attitude."

"There's no need for that, Marko," Alonee advised.

"Your old man's a firefighter, Alonee," Marko shot back, turning on the girl like a snapping dog. "Big deal. My father's gonna own the whole hood pretty soon. He's gonna have the power. Politicians gonna listen to him 'cause he's got the cash, y'hear what I'm sayin'? He's gonna have a say on the school board—who gets hired and who gets fired at Tubman. It's all about money, dudes. Guys like old Myers better watch their backs."

Jaris had been standing there listening. "Marko, you're wacko," he declared. "Just because some dude owns the local supermarket doesn't give him a say over the schools."

"We'll see," Marko warned. "Pretty soon, my father says 'jump,' everybody gonna say 'how high?' 'cause he's the man."

"Your father's a dirty cheat," a girl named Shatara Anderson announced suddenly. Jaris didn't know Shatara, though he'd seen her around the campus. A few times, Jaris and Shatara shared small talk around the vending machines. "Your father stole my grandpa's building," she accused. "He's a crook."

"What's that ugly chick sayin'?" Marko growled. "My father never stole anything!"

"My grandfather's old, and he don't think good no more," Shatara went on. "Your father and his crooked lawyers tricked him into selling his building for peanuts. Now when Grandpa dies, we won't get anything." The girl was near tears. "Your father's evil, Marko Lane."

Jaris remembered what old Jackson had told Pop about how Marko's father got the building he was going to use for a social club. Shatara's story rang true.

"You shut your dirty little mouth," Marko yelled at Shatara. "You're talkin' trash about the best man in this whole town. Everybody looks up to my father. He never cheated nobody. Your grandfather's gotta be nuts if he says my father cheated him."

Alonee put her hand on Shatara's arm. "Calm down," she advised. "Couple of the teachers are looking this way. They think there's gonna be a fight or something with all the yelling and screaming."

"His kind always win," Shatara remarked bitterly. "My parents work hard, and Grandpa always said he'd leave them that property when he passed. Now all the money Grandpa got is barely enough to bury him!"

Jaris had never seen Marko so upset. He worshipped his father. To listen to someone like Shatara throwing around words like "crook" and "cheat" hurt him deeply. Marko got along all right with his mother, but he had made an idol of his father.

Jaris drove over to the Manley house around the time Olivia Manley was leaving with her family. Jaris wanted to show his support. Sereeta said it'd be all right if he came. In fact, Sereeta told him, she would appreciate a hug from him to keep up her courage. The good-bye at the rehab center would probably be a tough one.

Olivia Manley was sitting in the living room, very sober, wearing a lovely powder blue suit. She looked beautiful. Jaris could see where Sereeta got her beauty.

Jaris walked over to her, hoping she did not have hard feelings about his visit the day before. But Mrs. Manley, if she remembered the visit at all, seemed please to see Jaris. He told her how Chelsea recalled her long-ago kindness in helping her clean up the chocolate ice cream on her dress. "Chelsea said she'll never forget how nice you were," Jaris told Olivia Manley.

Sereeta's mother smiled. She seemed very tense.

"Please tell Chelsea that is most sweet of her," the woman replied kindly.

Mrs. Manley's gaze flitted about the room for a second. Jaris was thinking about what he might say next, but Sereeta's mom spoke first.

"I want to get well, Jaris," she told him. "I want that more than anything."

"And you're going to girl," her sister Gayla chimed in. "We need to get back to hangin' out together and playin' tennis. You're my little sister. Nothin's gonna stop you from getting yourself back, girl."

Perry Manley stood back as Gayle and Artie Chandler walked to their car with Sereeta and her mother. Sereeta was holding her mother's hand very tightly. "Mom," she asserted, "when you get home, we're going to San Francisco again, like before. I've got the little cable car you got me in my bedroom. It's my favorite thing."

"I hope so," Olivia Manley responded. "I hope we can go again . . ."

"I'm sure of it, Mom," Sereeta assured her. Sereeta sounded so strong. Jaris was proud of her. She wasn't yet seventeen, but she seemed older, more confident than her mother. In fact, she seemed to be the mother, and Olivia Manley seemed to be the frightened child.

"We'll spend a couple days in the Bay Area, Mom," Sereeta went on. "We'll eat at those wonderful Italian restaurants we missed before. We'll see all the sights we didn't have time for before."

"Oh, I'd love that, Sereeta!" her mother sighed.

At the car, Jaris briefly took Sereeta in his arms and kissed her. Her eyes sparkled with tears. "Keep the faith, babe," Jaris commanded.

Artie Chandler shook hands with Jaris and commented about how big he was since the last time they met. He told Jaris to give his best to Pop. Maybe they'd be playing some pool next time he came to town. Gayla Chandler gave Jaris a motherly hug and thanked him for all he was doing for Sereeta.

Sereeta and her mother got into the backseat of the car, and the Chandlers got into the front. Then the car headed west to the rehab center.

As Jaris walked back to his own car, he happened to glance at the Manley house. He noticed a figure in the upstairs bedroom window. It was a man, holding a baby in his arms. They were a heartbreaking sight—Perry Manley and his son.

Jaris didn't really know Perry Manley. What little he knew he saw through the eyes of Sereeta, and it wasn't good. She never liked her stepfather, and he never liked her—a sad situation.

But, Jaris figured, he probably had some good in him. He had married beautiful Olivia Prince, a newly divorced woman, and they'd made a baby together, little Jake. At the time Jake was conceived, they both thought they wanted their own child. Now Jake was being raised mostly by nannies, but still he was their son. Perry Manley, for all his flaws, was sadly watching the baby's mother being taken off to a rehab center. He stayed with his son, holding the little one in his arms. And he didn't know—nobody knew—how or when this would all end.

Jaris drove home, feeling sad and forlorn. Sereeta had promised to call him tonight when she got back from the rehab center—no matter how late. The Chandlers would bring her home to her grandmother's house. Jaris needed to hear from her. He wanted to hear that her mother was settled in and that everything looked promising.

Jaris went home and tried to do some of the reading for Ms. McDowell's AP class. He found himself reading page after page and not getting a thing. His mind seemed to be skipping over the words like a car tire on an icy road. He couldn't focus. His mind was swirling.

"Hey boy, how's it goin'?" Pop asked, sticking his head in the doorway to Jaris's room.

"I dunno, Pop," Jaris murmured. "Sereeta went with her mom to the rehab. I could see Sereeta's stepdad standing in the upstairs window with the baby. It was sad."

Pop sighed. "I remember the night we went over there," he recalled. "'Member? Olivia, she was sitting there holding the baby, and she was pretty tanked up. I talked harsh to her. I told her she had to shape up. I guess I talked like a fool. When that stuff gets a hold of you, you can't climb out of the hole by yourself."

Pop sighed, recalling his own past. "I was lucky. I drank too much sometimes, but it never really took over my life. Maybe in a few more years, if I kept goin', I woulda had a big problem. Thank the Lord I never had to find out."

Jaris knew what Pop was talking about. But that was all in the past.

"Pop," the boy asked, "do you think they can help her? I never knew anybody who went to rehab like that."

"I had a buddy once," Pop responded. "He had a couple of DUIs, and they made him do rehab. He got clean, Jaris. My pop, your grandpa, he drank way too much. I used to go to the bars with him, and he'd slip me a drink. It wasn't legal, but he did it. You never knew your grandpa, Jaris. He died before you were two."

Pop's eyes stared off into the past. "You'd of liked him when he was sober. He played the trumpet like Louis Armstrong. That was before your time—even before my time. He had big dreams for me, Jare. I was the only boy. I was gonna be the big success story in the Spain line."

Pop's voice stalled for a few seconds. He looked deep in thought, then he went on. "He didn't take it too good when my college dreams fell through. He got mad at first. He blamed me for gettin' hurt and ruinin' my chances for the scholarship. He called me a 'stupid idiot.' But he got sorry then that he said that. He loved me a lot. He was disappointed, though. He wanted his boy to be somebody. He'd see me working on cars, earning good money. I'd show him my pay stubs. I'd say, 'Not bad, huh Pop?'. But in his eyes, I could see he was disappointed. He wanted more. He wanted to be really proud of me. . . . And he wasn't. He wasn't ever."

Pop looked off into the distance again.

Jaris thought this was where the darkness began, in his own father's disappointed eyes. This was where Pop learned that being "only a grease monkey," as he described himself, meant bitter failure.

"You know Jaris," Pop mused. "I wish my pop could see my garage, the big letters painted there: 'Spain's Auto Care.' I wish he'd lived long enough to see that anyway. Maybe, you know . . . maybe he does, huh boy? You think the old man is finally grinning from somewhere? Maybe he's thinkin', 'Lorenzo, he didn't do so bad after all.'" A faint smiled danced on Pop's lips.

"Yeah, Pop," Jaris assured him. "He is."

After Pop left the room, Jaris thought about his grandfather. He had a picture of him, a handsome man with a friendly face. When he was only fifty-seven years old, he collapsed on the street on his way to his janitor job downtown. He drank sometimes, but that morning he was sober. He drank only when he wasn't working. The police got there after a while and picked him up. They thought he was just another drunk after a night of celebrating nothing. Then they realized he was having a heart attack.

They got him to a hospital, but he didn't survive the day. He had worked very hard all his life and never paid attention to the symptoms sneaking up on him. At the time of his death, nobody paid much attention to high blood pressure, to good and bad diets, or to cholesterol levels.

At Grandpa's funeral, Pop had told Jaris once, someone from his father's barber shop group played the clarinet. The man played sweetly and beautifully. Pop's mother died two years later, leaving Lorenzo and Lita, his sister, without parents. Lita married a nice man and now had four kids. Last year when she had back surgery, Pop went up there to be with her. Jaris often heard Pop chatting with Lita on the phone. Every summer, Lita and her family came down to visit, or the Spains went north to see them.

Jaris was dozing when Jaris's phone rang at eleven o'clock.

"Hi," Sereeta said softly, "I'm home."

"How'd it go, babe?" Jaris asked, at first sleepily. "I wish I was with you right now. I'd give you a hug."

"I'd like that," Sereeta told him. "It went okay. The rooms are really nice. The staff seemed good. It seems more like a hotel than a *facility*. We helped Mom unpack her stuff and, you know, settle in. She's very hopeful."

"How long is she gonna be there?" Jaris asked.

"They aren't sure . . . maybe a month or more," Sereeta answered.

"That long?" Jaris said. But then he remembered that Sereeta's mother had had the addiction for a long time. You couldn't just blow it away over a weekend.

"Of course, she can leave any time she wants to," Sereeta added. "It's strictly voluntary, but she promised Aunt Gayla she'd stay as long as it took to help her. We visited with her for a coupla hours, and she seemed okay. But then, when we had to leave, she got sad. Her eyes got real big, and she said, 'I want to go home with you guys.' She just about broke my heart. I felt so bad leaving her there. All the way back in the car with Aunt Gayla and Uncle Artie, I had such a lump in my throat I couldn't talk."

"I know, babe. It had to be hard," Jaris consoled her.

"I guess we better get to sleep now, Jaris. School tomorrow, huh?" Sereeta suggested. "The beat goes on . . ."

"Yeah, Myers has scheduled a quiz already," Jaris replied. "Thanks for calling, Sereeta. See ya in the morning."

"Jaris," Sereeta said suddenly, "she seemed so small. I hugged her before we left the rehab place, and she seemed so . . . tiny. I mean, I weigh a hundred and ten, and I don't think she weighs a hundred pounds anymore. I could feel her ribs, Jaris. I don't think she's been eating much. Perry's been gone as much as possible, just to be away from the . . . stuff. And Mom's just been drinking."

"They'll make sure she eats healthy there, Sereeta," Jaris assured her. "Just try to trust the folks there. It'll be okay."

Jaris was dead tired. He needed to sleep. But Sereeta sounded so depressed that he talked to her for another ten minutes before she finally closed the phone. Then he turned over and tried to sleep.

Jaris lay there in the dark, worrying about Sereeta. At the same time, thoughts about AP American History and Mr. Myers's quiz tomorrow swirled in his head. Then he slept fitfully.

In the middle of a dream, he heard the wail of sirens. The sirens became part of his dream. He was out on the street, and there was an accident. People were yelling and screaming. It was one of the worst night-mares Jaris ever had.

Jaris opened his eyes and stared at his clock. It was two in the morning. Then he actually heard the sirens. *It was real*. Something had happened nearby. Maybe it was an accident, a crime, something bad. But now the sirens grew quiet. Jaris turned over again and tried to sleep. But now he couldn't.

# CHAPTER FIVE

Early the next morning, Jaris was just getting out of bed. His mother knocked and came into his room. She had a stricken look on her face, as if she brought bad news.

"Jaris," Mom said, "Dawna Lennox just called. Marko Lane was attacked last night with a baseball bat. For some reason, he was out jogging in the early hours of the morning, and he was hit. He's been taken to the hospital."

"*What?*" Jaris gasped. He couldn't wrap his mind around what Mom had just said. The sirens that seemed part of his dream—that was it. He must have really heard the sirens. Because he was not fully awake, he thought they were part of his dream. The attack had to have happened nearby.

"He's okay, isn't he, Mom?" Jaris asked. He felt numb. He'd wanted to strangle Marko Lane so many times, but this news shocked and troubled him.

"Dawna talked to his mother," Mom responded. "He was rushed into the emergency room around three o'clock. Dawna didn't know what his condition was."

"What happened?" Jaris asked. "I mean, did somebody just attack him, or was there a fight, or . . ."

"We don't know," Mom replied. "Just that he was attacked by someone with a baseball bat. Dawna is trying to find out if there's anything we can do. Marko's parents must be devastated."

When Jaris got out to the kitchen and sat down, Pop and Chelsea were already there. Pop sat at the table shaking his head.

"This kid's made so many enemies ever since he was little," Pop declared, "bullying other kids, stealing their lunches! You remember, Jaris, how he made you give him your orange every day. Then I got wind of it, and I scared the livin' daylights outta him. And as he got older, seems like he got meaner, mocking kids, taunting them. But what was he doin' running around on the streets at two in the morning? That's what I'd like to know."

"He's on the track team, Pop," Jaris explained. "Sometimes they do that. Trevor and Kevin do it too. It's too hot when the sun's up to run, and they go out when it's dark. The early morning hours are the best 'cause the streets are empty. Even the gangbangers've packed it in for the night."

Jaris remembered what Sami Archer had said just a few days ago: *If Marko turned up dead in an alley, the police would have to question half the kids at Tubman.*

"You think he's gonna die?" Chelsea asked, wide-eyed.

"No," Jaris said without conviction. "They'll be able to . . . you know . . . do something."

"You think it was somebody from school who did it?" Chelsea asked.

"I don't know, chili pepper," Jaris responded. "But I'm sure it's none of my friends. No way any of them could have done it. I mean, Marko has given us all reason to hate him. Me, Trev, Kevin, Oliver—all of us. But none of my friends are such cowards that they'd waylay a guy with a baseball bat."

"Coulda just been a random thing," Pop suggested. "Lotsa weirdoes out there on the street at night. You see them pushing their shopping carts, talking to themselves, yellin' at shadows. They're in a world of their own. You look at 'em sometimes, and they look real spaced out."

Jaris's phone rang, and he took the call.

"Hey, Jaris," Trevor Jenkins asked, "you heard?"

"About Marko, yeah," Jaris replied.

"Man, that's awful, huh," Trevor commented. "He was out there runnin' to get ready for our first track meet."

"I figured that's what he was doing," Jaris agreed.

"Yeah," Trevor continued, "Marko was just real determined to get in a lot of practice. He wanted to beat me and Kevin at the track meet, and, you know, impress his father. He was runnin' like a madman, sweatin' even though it was pretty cool."

"Trevor, what're you saying?" Jaris gasped. "You *saw* the dude running last night?"

"Yeah, Jaris. I was doin' the same thing," Trevor explained. "I started out from my house around one. Ma didn't even wake up. I sneaked out of the house and started runnin'. I saw Marko around one thirty. He was going down Pequot Street, and he looked drained. But he had this sneer on his face, like he's like gonna whip my tail. He yelled at me and said he was gonna leave me in his dust at the meet. He was talkin' trash, man, but I just kept runnin'. I pretended like I didn't even hear him. I swear I didn't even break my stride, man."

Trevor's voice was coming in nervous gulps. "And then, later," Trevor went on, "I heard the sirens but didn't think anything of it. Then this morning, the news said that he'd been whacked. Man, my blood ran cold. I was out there on Pequot Street like right before he got whacked. *What if somebody saw me?*"

"Trevor, what are the chances, at one-thirty in the morning, that somebody saw you?" Jaris asked.

"I don't know, man," Trevor answered. "But I was coming on Pequot Street, and this car passed me. The guy yells out the car window, 'Look out! You wanna get killed?' or something like that. What if it was somebody who knows me? Man, I'm sweatin' ice, Jaris. Marko musta gotten hit real close to there, and I was almost on top of it. I mean, everybody knows I hated Marko ever since I was first going with Vanessa. He even ratted me out to my ma."

"Take it easy, man," Jaris soothed him. "We all have a problem with Marko. Probably the guy who saw you never thought twice about it. Anyway, just 'cause you're jogging on the same street as Marko doesn't mean you did it."

"But what if the dude in the car tells the cops he saw me right there," Trevor asked.

"Stay cool, dude. It's okay," Jaris told him. "Just calm down. I'll see you in a little while at school. Okay?"

"Okay, man," was all Trevor could say.

Jaris closed the phone and looked up at his parents. "Marko and Trevor were both running on Pequot Street early this morning," Jaris told them. "They both had the same idea. Use the cool morning hours to practice for the track meet. Seems they ran into each other and Marko dissed Trevor as usual, but Trevor just ignored him. Now Trev is freakin'. He's afraid somebody saw him out there around the time Marko got hit and they're gonna blame him."

"That's crazy," Pop protested. "Trevor's a good kid. Nobody's gonna think he'd do something like that."

"It's so dangerous for those boys to be running at night," Mom remarked, "or even in the morning when it's dark. I'm glad you're not on the track team, Jaris."

Jaris's thoughts were elsewhere. He was worried about Trevor. He knew Trevor well enough to know he'd never hit anybody over the head with a baseball bat, even somebody he hated. But not everybody knew Trevor that well. To a stranger, Trevor was a big, rough kid who'd had his share of trouble. He was mixed up with Vanessa Allen and her creepy friends. What if that guy in the car recognized Trevor and told the police about a dude close to where Marko was hit? They might get ideas.

Jaris barely ate his breakfast. He could not get Marko off his mind. He was worried about Trevor getting caught up in the thing. He thought maybe Trevor would be better off going to the police. He could simply tell them he'd been running and he saw Marko running too. He just wanted to let them know. Otherwise, if the police learned from somebody else that Trevor was so close to the crime, Trevor might look guilty.

Then again, Jaris wasn't sure. Maybe the guy in the car didn't even know Trevor. Why should Trevor volunteer information that would put him close to a brutal crime, possibly a murder?

Jaris was putting his stuff in his binder for school when Pop pushed back from the table. "Well, time for me to get down to the zoo," he announced. "The new kid's coming today. I'm breakin' in Darnell Meredith. Gotta introduce him to all the old beaters that I've been keepin' goin' since before he was born." Pop stuck on his LA Dodgers baseball cap and was heading for the door when Mom stopped him.

"Lorenzo," she asked, "I wonder if we know what we got?"

"Come again, babe?" Pop responded.

"I mean, what just happened to Marko," Mom commented. "In a second's time, it can all be taken away. Our lives, they're so good now, Lorenzo. The kids are healthy, and they're doing well. We're healthy. A little bit older but still good to go. You got the garage. I'm excited about my new classes. Someday we'll look back on these times and wonder why we weren't bursting with happiness. I'm just so grateful to be here right now with you and the kids."

"That's good thinkin', Monie," Pop agreed. "Real good thinkin'. Tell you what. Let's stop and enjoy this moment just a little bit."

Jaris peered around the corner, but he didn't need to. His parents were in each other's arms, hugging tightly, rocking slightly back and forth. Jaris smiled, turned down the hallway, and rapped on Chelsea's bedroom door.

"Time to go, chili pepper!" he called.

"My hair won't work," Chelsea groaned. "It's all sticking out."

"Push it back in, chili pepper," Jaris told her. "We gotta get goin'."

"Ohhh!" Chelsea whined. The door opened, and she had her backpack ready. She followed Jaris out to the car.

As they rode to school, Chelsea was saying something about Athena's parents fighting all the time. Then she complained about Inessa being such a wet blanket. But Jaris paid no attention to her chatter.

He was thinking about Trevor. He was tormenting himself with what-ifs. What if Trevor had not told Jaris the entire truth? What if Marko and Trevor had met on Pequot Street? What if Marko taunted Trevor, maybe about Vanessa Allen, and Trevor lost it? What if Trevor carried a baseball bat when he jogged at such a dangerous hour? In one blind moment of rage, normal people do terrible things. Jaris had seen the rage in Trevor's eyes the day before, after Marko had busted him.

"I bet Pop was right," Chelsea piped up just before they got to Tubman. "I bet somebody just hit Marko 'cause they were crazy or something. I see those guys sleeping behind the dumpsters. Some of them are on drugs and stuff. They look real wild. Maybe Marko made fun of one of them, and he jumped out and attacked Marko. Marko shouldn't all the time be making fun of people."

"You're right about that, chili pepper," Jaris agreed.

"I hope Marko gets better," Chelsea added. "I know he's mean and everything, but I don't want him to die. It makes me sad to think he might die. I've never known anybody who died. I know that drug dealer, B.J. Brady died, but I didn't know him. Marquis, a boy in fifth grade, got leukemia. We thought he was gonna die, but he didn't. Now all his hair came back and everything. He's here at Tubman now, and he said 'Hi' to me. It made me fool good all over."

"I hope Marko gets better too, chili pepper," Jaris told her.

"Honest?" Chelsea asked in a serious voice. "'Cause I know he's been mean to Sereeta, and that hurts you a lot. I thought maybe you hated him a lot."

"I hate him when he does something rotten, Chelsea," Jaris admitted. "A coupla times I wanted to just have a go at him, man to man. Couple times it almost happened. But I don't hate him deep down. I keep hoping he'll change and become a decent guy."

When Jaris dropped Chelsea off at school, he noticed Alonee and Sami talking in front of Harriet Tubman's statue. He joined them.

"Bad stuff, huh?" Jaris commented.

"I knew that boy would run into trouble the way he acts," Sami declared. "He just too mean for his own good. I hated to hear it, though. When Alonee's Mom called us, I like to have fainted. I even got the shakes so bad I couldn't eat breakfast."

Alonee reported to Jaris. "My mom's down at the hospital now. Sami's mom too.

Marko's parents need some support right now."

"How's he doing?" Jaris asked. "Anybody know?"

"Last I heard he was in the ICU," Alonee replied. "He got hit bad. Mom and Mrs. Archer are going to stay with the Lanes until the doctors come out and talk to them."

"It must be terrible for his parents," Jaris remarked. Trevor Jenkins was usually at the statue by this time, but Jaris didn't see him. He hoped Trevor hadn't freaked out and decided to stay home from school. If he got involved in the investigation, that kind of behavior wouldn't help him.

Then Derrick Shaw and Destini Fletcher came walking toward the small group.

"Somebody got him, huh?" Derrick asked. "I caught a lot of stuff from Marko. Maybe I caught more 'cause I'm not the sharpest knife in the drawer. He sure liked to point that out. But I never wanted anything bad to happen to the guy. I'm real sorry about this."

Alonee glanced at the arriving students. She announced, "Jasmine and her parents went down to the hospital too. Mom talked to Mrs. Benson. She says Jasmine is so hysterical that the doctor had to give her a sedative. Jasmine said she went out with Marko last night, and then he took her home. He told Jasmine he had to practice running so he could blow away the competition in the track meet. Jasmine told him not to run too late, but he just laughed. He said he wasn't afraid of the dark."

Jaris didn't see Kevin Walker around either. His girlfriend, Carissa Polson, came along, though. "Hey, Carissa," Jaris hailed. "You seen Kevin?"

Carissa smiled and shook her head. "He's late sometimes. He's a sorta bad boy."

"You hear what happened to Marko, Carissa?" Alonee asked. Carissa shook her head no. Alonee said, "Somebody hit him over the head with a baseball bat. He's hurt bad."

Carissa looked shocked. Then she commented, "He's been so mean, like to Kevin. I guess something had to happen to him."

Oliver Randall had shown up with a group of students. He'd heard what Alonee said, and he looked grim. "I remember Marko dissing my dad. I saw red. I almost hit him then, but Kevin Walker stopped me. I've always been grateful for that. Who knows what might've happened?"

Shatara Anderson walked up then, pure glee on her face. "You guys hear about old Chuck Lane's pride and joy? He's probably gonna die. Serves the old man right for cheating my family."

"Shatara," Sami Archer commanded, putting her hand on the girl's arm, "you don't want to be talkin' like that. Makes no difference how much you hurt."

Shatara moved Sami's hand aside. "What do you know, Sami?" Shatara sneered. "He didn't ruin *your* family. You shoulda seen my parents when they found out the property was gone. My father, he sits in a chair and cries kinda like a child. He turns into an old man *right before my eyes*. He's broken. Chuck Lane and his dirty gold chains, he did it. Now he's probably gonna have to bury his only son. Serves him right."

"That *would* be weird, huh," Derrick remarked. "If what happened to Marko had nothin' to do with his own sins. Shatara has a lotta hate in her. Maybe other folks hired somebody to whack Marko to get back at his father."

Jaris kept looking around for Kevin and Trevor. They were Marko's big rivals on the track team. Trevor was probably staying home from school because he was so scared. He was worried that somebody saw him on Pequot Street around the time Marko was attacked. Trevor was weak in some ways. His mother, Mickey Jenkins, had raised good boys on her own, without a husband. But in some sad way, by being so strong herself, she made them weak in some ways.

Before going to his first class, Jaris called Kevin on his cell phone. No answer. Then Jaris called Kevin's grandparents, whom he lived with. He called them on their home phone.

"Hi, this is Jaris Spain, Kevin's friend from Tubman," Jaris began. "I haven't seen Kevin in school today, and I was sorta worried. Is he home sick or something?" Jaris asked.

Kevin's grandfather had answered the phone. He was a little hard of hearing. "You callin' from the school? Who's this? You the teacher?" he asked.

Jaris spoke a little louder and more slowly. "This is Jaris Spain. I'm a friend of Kevin's. He's not here at school today, and I was worried. Is he home sick?"

"No, he ain' sick," the old man replied. "Me and his grandma worried too. He ain' been around here since yesterday mornin'. Ain' like the boy to just take off like that without sayin' nothin'. We been callin' him on that phone he carries around. But some voice keeps on puttin' us on what they call 'voice mail' or somethin'."

Jaris took a deep breath.

"I'll keep an eye out for him, Mr. Stevens," Jaris promised Kevin's grandfather. "I'll call you if I see him."

"Hold on, boy. Grandma wants to talk to you," Roy Stevens said. "Here Lena, here's the phone."

"Jaris? Jaris Spain?" Lena Stevens asked.

"Yes, Mrs. Stevens," Jaris answered. "I'm here."

"I'm real worried, Jaris," the woman confided. "Kevin been keepin' things from us here lately. He say he's gone on a date with Carissa. Then we call her, and he's not with her. He been sneakin' around and lyin' to us. I'm real scared, Jaris. You know all about his daddy and what he done and all. We all the time hopin' and prayin' it don' come to that with this boy. We love him with all our hearts. And we're so afraid."

"I'm sure he's okay, Mrs. Stevens," Jaris assured Grandma. "He's just kinda moody sometimes. But I'll let you know the minute I see him."

"Please let us know if you learn anythin', Jaris?" The old woman sounded as though she was pleading.

"I will, ma'am," Jaris promised. "Don't worry. He's fine. Good-bye now."

Jaris knew why Kevin was making up stories to his grandparents. He was learning to box, something they would never approve of. As for the last day or so, he might have just caught a bus to the next town to watch a boxing match. Kevin Walker was an impulsive guy.

And Kevin was into boxing. His dad had been an excellent boxer. In fact, he had had a real shot at going to the Olympics with the American team and winning the gold. But he got into a fight instead and killed a man. He went to prison, where he died in a prison riot. His dad's death haunted Kevin. He lived in his father's shadow and bore his father's violent temper.

Kevin struggled with his fiery temper, drawing back from fights at the last minute. He thought boxing might help him control himself. Kevin often went to spar at a gym about five miles away. He never told his grandparents any of this, though. They were his mother's parents, and they never liked Kevin's father. Their son-in-law had broken their daughter's heart and left her with a son to raise alone. When she died, the grandparents took over the strange boy they desperately loved and fretted over.

Kevin told Jaris that controlling his temper was his biggest challenge. Once Kevin almost did attack Marko. But, as Kevin once told Jaris, his dead mother's voice warned him off. Maybe, Jaris thought, Kevin had tangled with Marko once again. And this time, no one was around to stop him.

But he wouldn't use a baseball bat, Jaris thought. Hand-to-hand fighting, that was something Kevin Walker might do. But a baseball bat against another guy's head? No way, Jaris thought. Kevin would have no part of that.

# CHAPTER SIX

That same day, Chelsea joined her friends for lunch again. Everybody came but Heston, who was trying out for the track team.

"Some senior guy from here got attacked last night on Pequot Street," Falisha reported. "I bet your brother knows him, huh, Chelsea?"

"Jaris knows him, yeah," Chelsea replied. "But they're not friends. Hardly anybody likes the guy who was hurt—Marko Lane. He's always making people feel bad. Like if a girl weighs a little too much, he'll make fun of her."

"Your brother is a pretty tough character," Maurice remarked. "He wasn't the one who whacked that Marko Lane, was he?"

Chelsea frowned. "Maurice! Jaris is a good guy. He wouldn't hurt anybody like that. Hitting somebody in the head with a baseball bat is like trying to murder them."

"Is the dude gonna die or what?" Inessa asked.

"We don't know yet," Chelsea answered. "Jaris promised me he'd call on my cell phone if he found out anything while we're at lunch."

Athena lay back on the grass and looked up at the sky. It was filled with fleecy clouds. "Know what?" she commented. "My father was coming back from a business trip last night. He was driving down Pequot Street, where that guy was attacked. My dad came through there about two or something. He saw a guy running, and he almost ran in front of my father's car. My dad, he yelled at him."

"You think that was Marko Lane before he got attacked?" Keisha asked.

"Maybe, or maybe it was the guy who attacked him," Athena suggested. "My father called the police this morning when we heard what happened. He told the police that this dude was running on Pequot Street."

"Wow!" Falisha exclaimed. "Maybe your father was the last one to see that Marko Lane alive!"

"Maybe he's not gonna die, Falisha," Chelsea said.

"I bet he is," Inessa insisted. "You know how hard those bats are? I bet he's in awful shape."

"Somebody musta hated that Marko Lane a lot to do that to him," Falisha remarked. "I don't like that guy my mom hangs with, that Shadrach. But I don't hate him."

"Good for you, Falisha," Chelsea said. "'Cause you shouldn't hate anybody, and Shadrach is really nice."

Chelsea's cell phone started playing her favorite rap song, and she grabbed it. "Yeah, Jaris? What's the scoop on Marko?"

"Marko has a concussion and a real bad laceration on his head, chili pepper," Jaris reported. "But he looks good. Whoever whacked him got off this one hard blow, then apparently took off. Marko's gonna be moved to a regular room in the hospital today. He'll be out of intensive care."

"Oh, Jaris," Chelsea cried, "I'm so glad! I didn't want him to die."

"Me neither, chili pepper," Jaris agreed. "I mean, who'd make our lives miserable on the Tubman campus? What if we didn't have Marko Lane? We'd be lost."

Chelsea giggled and gave the news to her friends. "You guys like my ring tone?" she asked. "I just put it on. It's a new hip-hop song from the Blastin' Caps."

Jaris stuffed his phone in his pocket and headed for the eucalyptus trees. That was where he and Alonee's posse ate as juniors. Now they claimed it again as seniors. As Jaris came down the path, Alonee and Oliver, Derrick and Destini, and Sami Archer were all there. "I just got off the phone with your mom, Alonee," Jaris advised. "Looks like our friend is gonna live."

Sami laughed. "The Lord don't want him, and the devil won't take him neither. So what do you do? Look like we're stuck with the boy." She was joking, but she seemed genuinely relieved.

For better or worse, most of Jaris's close friends could not remember a time when Marko Lane was not giving them trouble. Marko was often a thorn in their sides—a pain—but a familiar figure.

"It wouldn't seem right not to have him around, stirring up trouble," Alonee remarked. "I mean, for just about my whole life, Marko's been running people down. He's done nothing but cause fights and just mess up our lives. Now, when it looked for a while like we might never see him again, it was . . . I don't know . . . *sad.*"

Oliver grinned. "I was looking forward to him fawning over Mr. Myers's poetry again. I really like seeing Myers put him down. It was just getting interesting. It didn't seem fair that he should be gone."

Derrick laughed too. "He hassled me so much, I kinda got used to it. I wonder if being hurt like this'll make him different. You know, like sometimes when something big happens, people look at life different. Their lives kinda go before their eyes, and they change. But I guess that won't happen with Marko," Derrick sighed.

"He won't be any different," Destini predicted. "He'll probably be even meaner."

Just then, Kevin Walker came down the path with his sandwich.

"Hey dude!" Jaris called to him. "Call your grandparents. They're worried about you. Seems like you've been a missing person for a while."

"Yeah, I called them. My car broke down," Kevin responded.

"You heard didn't you, Kevin?" Oliver asked. "Marko Lane almost got murdered."

"Oh yeah?" Kevin replied without emotion. "How'd that happen?"

"Somebody whacked him over the head with a baseball bat last night on Pequot Street," Alonee explained. "He was practice running for the track meet. He's in the hospital now. He's got a concussion, but Jaris says he's going to be all right."

"Oh man!" Kevin commented flatly. "I'm sure glad to hear that. How could we have lived around here without that puke?"

Alonee and Jaris exchanged a troubled look.

"I've been taking boxing lessons over at the gym, you know," Kevin announced. He seemed disinterested in Marko's misfortune. He didn't even ask if they knew who did it. "My father was an excellent boxer, but I'm just getting started. Trainer thinks I got talent. I'm really enjoying it too. Don't any of you guys tell my grandparents, though. They didn't like anything about my dad, including him being a fighter. They'd freak if they thought I was following in his footsteps."

"I like watching boxing matches," Derrick remarked.

"I don't," Destini disagreed. "They're too brutal."

"It's not brutal when you have style like Muhammad Ali had," Kevin objected. "I've watched films of his fights. 'Float like a butterfly, sting like a bee!' Talk about grace." Kevin finished his sandwich. "Well, I gotta go make excuses for missing math this morning." He got up and went up the path.

There was an uneasy silence when he was gone.

"He's sure not a fan of Marko's," Oliver declared.

"None of us are, but with him it runs really deep," Alonee said. "He had such a hard look in his eyes."

"Marko really hurt him bad," Jaris recalled. "Remember, Kevin was trying to keep his past secret, about his dad in prison and stuff. Marko found out, and he made Kevin's life miserable. Marko hated Kevin anyway because he's such a good runner. He thought he could throw him off his stride by tormenting him about his dad. Marko even stuck an ugly limerick about it on Kevin's locker. Kevin went berserk. I didn't blame him either. Some things you just can't forgive."

Jaris was wondering whether Kevin was really at the gym last night. Or was he out running around Pequot Street too? Maybe, Jaris thought, Marko and Kevin tangled. Maybe something snapped in Kevin.

Jaris glanced at Oliver and Alonee. Their faces had strange looks too, as if they were thinking the same thing. Nobody wanted to come right out and say what they were all thinking, though. Everybody liked Kevin too much even to hint he might have done something that awful, even if he was provoked.

At the end of the school day, Jaris waited for his sister. Jaris waited as usual by the Honda while she finished talking with her friends. Today she was even later than usual. Jaris looked at all the freshmen girls coming briskly along. He wondered why Chelsea had to be the last one out of the chute.

Finally, he and Chelsea were in the car. Chelsea related what Athena had said about her dad being on Pequot last night. Before driving off, Jaris called Trevor on his cell.

"Man, why'd you miss school today?" Jaris asked.

"My mind is so messed up, I couldn't take it," Trevor explained. "I told Ma I had a bad stomach ache, and I kinda do. You hear anything about how Marko is doin'?"

"Yeah," Jaris replied. "He's got a concussion and a bad laceration. They moved him from the ICU, and he's in a regular room now. Looks like he's gonna make it."

"Man, that's good news," Trevor sighed with relief. "At least he's not dead. I wonder if he's told the cops who did it to him? I sure hope so. Then I'm off the hook."

"I don't know, Trev," Jaris answered. "I'm sure the police will question him when he's up to it. My guess is, somebody got him from behind. Marko's a strong guy. If somebody had come at him from the front, I think Marko could've wrestled the bat from the dude. I figure he was running in the dark, and somebody just came up behind him and hit him. Marko probably never saw it comin'."

"I sure wish he'd seen the guy," Trevor said.

"Trevor," Jaris began, "my sister heard something from a friend today. Her friend's father was coming home from a trip around the time Marko got hit. This guy said he almost hit a kid who was running in the street—across Pequot."

"That was me!" Trevor gasped. "That musta been the guy who yelled at me. Oh man! Did Chelsea say if he recognized me?"

"No, he didn't. He said it was just a kid," Jaris answered.

"If my ma got a whiff of any of this, she'd go ballistic, Jaris," Trevor remarked. "Everything I've gained of her trust would just go out the window. She's always been haunted by this fear of one of her boys going bad, ending up in jail. She's always said she'd rather have a dead son than one in prison."

"Dude, come to school tomorrow," Jaris urged. "It's the first week of school. You can't afford to miss any more classes."

"I hear you, man," Trevor admitted. "I'll be there. I feel a little better knowing Marko's gonna be okay. I can't stand the guy, but I don't want nobody dead. And I sure don't want to be blamed for it."

The boys ended the call. But before Jaris could start the car, Sami Archer came along. She was grinning at Jaris.

"This gonna be me next year, waitin' on Maya when she comes to Tubman," Sami chuckled. "But I'll have to come from the community college and pick her up. That's gonna be loads of fun. Maya's a motor-mouth, just like Chelsea. Not that I ain't."

Sami leaned on the roof of the car and talked to Jaris through the driver's side window. "Hey Jare, maybe we oughta be goin' down to the hospital and bringing Marko flowers."

Jaris laughed. "He'd throw them back at us, Sami. Right now he's probably thinking we're all celebrating that he got whacked. Unless he saw who hit him, he's probably sure it was one of us."

"Yeah, but if he's still in the hospital, I'm goin' down with Mom and Dad," Sami said. "Alonee is goin' with her parents too. You wanna come, Jaris? You can ride with us."

"No thanks, Sami," Jaris declined. "I really, *really* don't like the guy. I'm not as bighearted and forgiving as you guys are. You're some kind of an angel, and I'm not. That's why you were voted Princess of the Fair." Jaris held his hand to his chest and rolled his eyes toward heaven. Then he mockingly intoned, "You best exemplify the virtues of Harriet Tubman."

"Oh go on!" Sami scoffed, giving Jaris a slap on the shoulder. "I ain't no angel, but sometimes you gotta fake it, you know?"

"Gotta go, Sami," Jaris insisted. "Chelsea here, she talks all day with her friends, and then she's gotta talk some more before I get her into the car." Chelsea shot Jaris an annoyed look. "Then," Jaris went on, "she'll go home and text them all half the night."

"Jaris, you got any hunches about who whacked Marko?" Sami asked.

"No," Jaris answered too quickly.

"I'm worried about Kevin Walker," Sami remarked. "I didn't like the way he acted at lunch."

"But he never would've done something like that," Jaris objected. "A fistfight, a knockdown, drag-out fight maybe. But he'd never jump someone with a baseball bat. That's not him."

"Yeah, you're right, Jaris," Sami admitted.

Chelsea piped up. "Jare," she whined, "are we going or what?"

Jaris looked at Sami as if to say, "*Now* she's in a hurry." Sami chuckled and walked on to her car.

"Okay, chili pepper," he told his sister. "We want to get home before it's tomorrow, and we have to turn around and come back!"

When Chelsea and Jaris got home, Mom was already there. "I called Marko's mother to offer our sympathy. I asked her if there was anything we could do," Mom said. "I thought I ought to do that. I've talked to Marko's mother a few times when we ran into each other at the market."

"That was nice, Mom," Jaris commented.

"*She* wasn't, though," Mom responded.

"Wasn't *what*?" Jaris asked.

"Nice," Mom answered. "She was very cold and angry. She went on and on about how all the kids at Tubman abused her wonderful son and made his life miserable. She was saying she and her husband were so angry at how unfairly he's treated."

Jaris and Chelsea hadn't even put their books down. Still standing just inside the door, they looked wide-eyed at each other. Their thoughts were the same: "*We* make his life miserable?"

Mom went on. "They're thinking of sending him to a private school for his senior year."

Jaris clutched at his chest with his hand. He staggered a few steps. Finally, he exclaimed, "Oh, my heart be still!"

Chelsea giggled. Jaris, she thought, was getting to be a clown like Pop.

Mom just kept going. She glanced at Jaris and began speaking again. "That boy Marko has done so many cruel things to so many kids. Yet his mother wouldn't own any of that. Not that I brought it up at a time like this. But I think at last I understand why Marko is so mean and remorseless. His parents have never held him accountable for his ugly behavior."

Mom was beside herself. She finally had an audience for her fuming rant. "Mrs. Lane," Mom rattled on, "actually told me what a great student and model citizen Marko was. He's a great athlete and an asset to Tubman High. Yet everybody mistreats him, and now this. She almost came right out and said it was a conspiracy. She almost said that his enemies got together to hurt him. They picked somebody to sneak up behind Marko and hit him with a baseball bat."

"Oh brother!" Jaris groaned. "Is Marko conscious yet?"

"His mother said he was," Mom responded, "though he's still a little spacey. It seems like he has no idea who hit him. He was just running along on Pequot Street. Suddenly he felt this terrible blow, and he woke up in the hospital. I tried so hard to assure Mrs. Lane that our prayers and good wishes are with Marko and his family. But then you know what she said?" Mom seemed deeply sad and hurt. "She said, 'I'm sorry to say this, Mrs. Spain. But your son has been anything but kind to Marko. He is one of the worst offenders against my poor Marko.' "

Jaris couldn't help himself. " '*One* of the worst,' " he gasped? "Mom, I do my best. I always thought I was *the* worst."

Jaris shook his head in fake disappointment. Chelsea giggled again.

Mom looked at him disapprovingly, but the ghost of a smirk crossed her mouth.

Jaris changed over to being serious. "Mom," he explained, "you know that's not true. Marko's the meanest guy I know. For Pete's sake, he's the meanest guy any of us know. I just try to stick up for myself . . . and Sereeta."

Mom looked puzzled. Jaris started to explain. "On the first day of school, Marko was yelling at poor Sereeta, making fun of her mom. *On the very first day*. He's never forgiven Sereeta for refusing to date him and for being my girlfriend. The very same day, he called Oliver 'a freakin' oddball' because he knew something in class that nobody else did. Mom, it just goes on and on like that with Marko."

Pop came in then, smudged with oil and grease but happy. "Monie," he hailed his wife, "you were right. Darnell's a great kid. This one's a winner. He knows his stuff, and he's super with the customers. Polite and friendly, just like you want a kid to be. You're battin' a thousand with your advice so far, Monie. Thank you, ma'am, for the tip on him."

Then Pop's smile faded. He looked around at the gloomy faces. Suddenly, he feared the worst. "So . . . how's Marko Lane?"

"He's got a concussion and a bad cut, but he'll live," Jaris replied.

"I guess we should break out the bubbly and celebrate," Pop declared. "But I think I'll pass."

"He's a creep," Jaris agreed, "but I'm glad he's okay."

"Yeah," Pop said. "I talked to his old man once, the dude with the gold chains. His Lexus broke down right in front of our garage. He never woulda stopped at a little place like Jackson was runnin' then. But what could he do? In he comes, his gold chains sparkling, acting like the Duke of California. He wants his Lexus fixed *now*.

Never mind the beaters sittin' there ahead of him. Let those suckers wait."

Pop laughed. "Well, old Jackson, he wasn't havin' any of that. Jackson, he ain't no respecter of big shots. Y'hear what I'm sayin'? So Lane, he's gotta cool his heels and take his turn. So he starts spoutin' about his great kid, Marko. Oh, he's the fastest kid on the track team, straight A student. He's the most popular guy on campus, got the chicks fallin' over themselves to be with him."

"Sounds delusional," Mom remarked, frowning.

# CHAPTER SEVEN

Later, relaxing in his room, Jaris played some rap music on his iPod. He was trying to erase the events of the day. But a horrible thought crept into his mind. What if he *knew* Kevin was the one who attacked Marko? What would he do? Of course, the right and responsible thing to do would be to turn Kevin in. Could he do that? His head told him he would and could. His heart argued.

Jaris turned off the iPod and started doing some reading for AP American History. He had to get focused on the course. He wasn't focused yet, and, at this rate, he'd flunk in a heartbeat.

When Jaris got to sleep that night, he had one of the worst nightmares of his life.

He had arrived early at Tubman, and Chelsea had rushed off as usual to join her friends. Jaris stood at the statue of Harriet Tubman, and Kevin Walker came along.

"So, I guess you know," Kevin said in a calm voice. He had a strange, wild light in his eyes.

"Know what?" Jaris asked, but he didn't have to ask. He knew just what Kevin meant. It was about the crime against Marko.

"You know what happened, more or less," Kevin responded. "It's been coming for a long time."

"No, I don't know," Jaris protested, fighting off his inescapable thoughts. He knew, but he couldn't say he knew.

"We were all running that night," Kevin explained. "Me, Trevor, Marko. Marko and me ended up on the same street at the same time. He stopped me and yelled at me. It was the same-old-same-old, ragging on my father. He was talking trash big time. I knew it would happen eventually. Someday he would push me too far."

In the dream, Jaris saw Kevin and Marko in dark, on Pequot Street. Marko was badgering Kevin. Jaris could hear Kevin talking to him, like a voiceover in a movie.

"I was ready for him," Kevin went on. "I had this old bat with me. When I run late at night, I always carry a bat just in case somebody gives me trouble. You can't be too careful, man. Anyway, Marko, he was trying to undermine me for the track meet coming up. He thought dissing my father again would make me crazy, throw me off. I couldn't take it anymore. I ran off in a different direction, like I was going away. Then I circled back."

Jaris saw Kevin run off into the darkness. Marko yelled insults at Kevin, then turned and started running again.

"I waited for him," Kevin told Jaris. But now Jaris couldn't see him. He only heard his voice and saw Marko running. Then he saw Kevin emerge from the darkness behind Marko. "When he passed me, I came up behind him, and I did it. I hit him hard. It sounded like his head cracked open. That's what it sounded like."

"No!" Jaris protested. "Why did you have to tell me, man? Why did you do this to me?"

"I wanted to be rid of him," Kevin explained, as Marko lay in the street. "I thought you'd understand, Jaris. I didn't just do it for myself. He's been like a virus spreading his poison around Tubman. I did it for all of us. You're with me, right, Jaris?" The wild light in Kevin's eyes spread over his whole face. He looked unreal, like a comic book villain.

"Kevin, no, it was wrong man!" Jaris told him. "You can't do a thing like that. I don't care what kind of a creep Marko is. It wasn't right to whack him with a baseball bat and try to take him out."

"Don't matter now," Kevin responded. "I know you won't rat me out, dude. I know you won't." Kevin was grinning like a maniac. He reminded Jaris of the Joker in the Batman movies.

Jaris woke up with a start and sat bolt upright in bed. He was perspiring heavily. He was so grateful he was only dreaming. It was a crazy, impossible dream. Kevin was a good guy. He'd never do something like that—never. Jaris got out of bed, went into the bathroom, and threw cold water in his face. He stepped over to the window. There was a bright moon glow. It must have been like this the other night when Marko got hurt. Somebody had to have seen something.

When Jaris arrived at school the next day, Trevor Jenkins was waiting for him. "Dude, the cops came to the house last night," Trevor told him, his voice shaky. "Ma was like havin' a heart attack. She didn't now what was goin' on, man. Marko told the cops I was out there on Pequot Street that night. He said we had an argument, and then he didn't see me anymore. I think Marko kinda believes I'm the one who whacked him, Jaris. I admitted to the cops I was joggin' there. But I swore to them I never hit Marko. I'm afraid they're gonna arrest me, Jaris. They'll come here to the school and take me away. It'll kill Ma. *But I didn't do anything!*"

Jaris had never seen Trevor so distraught. "Calm down, Trevor," Jaris said. "Marko didn't tell the cops you whacked him, did he?"

"No," Trevor answered. "He said somebody came up behind him and did it. He never saw them. But he said he'd just seen me a few minutes earlier. And there's nobody else on that street at two in the morning. How many people out there? Just him and me. And he's sayin' we were fightin' and stuff, but that's a lie. He was just yellin' insults at me, and I was ignorin' him. But to the cops it makes sense that I doubled back and got him with the baseball bat."

Trevor was breathing heavily, almost sobbing. "Jaris, I can hardly think. I don't even know what I'm doin' in school today."

"Trevor, the cops have the baseball bat, right?" Jaris reasoned. "Your prints won't be on it. They can't pin this on you, man."

"I don't know. I guess," Trevor responded. "Jaris, you shoulda seen the look on Ma's face. Cops comin' in our house and questionin' her son. She's sittin' there, claspin' herself, rockin' back and forth. She's goin', 'Oh merciful Lord, save us!' I told her I didn't hurt Marko, and she believes me. She knows I'd never do anything like that. But I was right in the middle of it."

"Look Trevor," Jaris explained, "the cops had to talk to you. Marko told them you were there on Pequot Street. They had to come and talk to you, but it doesn't mean anything. They're not out to get you for something you didn't do."

"The cops," Trevor said, "they told me not to go anywhere, like out of town or something. Like I have a big trip planned or somethin'. They said they'll maybe wanna talk to me some more. I didn't like the way they were lookin' at me, Jaris. Marko and me, we weren't friends. Everybody knows that. There's bad blood between us."

"You and everybody else, Trevor," Jaris told him.

"Yeah, but I was the only one on Pequot Street that night he got whacked," Trevor insisted.

"Keep the faith, man!" Jaris told him, grabbing his friend for a hug. "You're gonna be all right. Trust me."

In Ms. Colbert's class, Chelsea was still thinking about the incident when she was scolded for whispering in class. She didn't think she had earned back her teacher's respect yet. But Chelsea still liked Ms. Colbert. She was one of the most animated and interesting teachers Chelsea ever had.

Toward the end of class, Ms. Colbert made an announcement. "We have some students working with Shadrach on the opossum rescue program. For them, we are planning a rescue caravan next Monday after dark. It will be about seven o'clock. If you want to participate, I'll pick you up at your homes as usual around six forty-five. You'll need signed permission slips from your parents."

Ms. Colbert held up a handful of permission slips. "You can ride in my van, and we'll follow Shadrach as he makes his rounds. What we do is cruise the streets looking for sick or wounded opossums in fields or by the side of the roads. You can count on being home by ten."

Chelsea looked over at Athena, and both girls raised their hands. Heston and Maurice raised their hands too. "Okay," Ms. Colbert smiled, "Chelsea, Athena, Heston, and Maurice. We've got our team of four. So remember, bring signed permission slips. Wear old, sturdy clothing in case we walk into the brush and, of course, sturdy shoes. Jeans and long-sleeved shirts are good. No dress-up."

Ms. Colbert was walking in the aisles handing permission slips to the four students. "The last time we went on one of these caravans," she continued, "we found two very badly hurt opossums. One had to be put down, but we saved the other. She was eventually released. Oh, and one more thing, keep writing in your journals. If you're not in the opossum project, pick an extra credit project. Choose one from the list I passed out on the first day of school. Everyone should have a chance to earn extra credit."

After class, Chelsea and Athena and the boys gathered outside. "That's gonna be exciting," Chelsea remarked. "Like a search and rescue mission."

"Yeah," Athena agreed, "Ms. Colbert just lights up when she talks about it. I think she likes being with Shadrach as much as she likes to rescue opossums!"

Chelsea giggled.

When Chelsea got home from school that day, Mom was at a faculty meeting at her school. Pop was home.

"Pop," Chelsea asked, "waddya doing home so early?"

"Darnell did great today," he answered. "And old Jackson is hangin' around doin' a little work too. I think he's bored at home since he sold the garage. I finally got some time off!"

"Pop, you gotta sign this permission slip," Chelsea told him, "so we can go rescue opossum this Monday night."

"I gotta sign what, little girl?" Pop asked, his eyebrows going up. "I don't gotta sign anything. What's this now?"

"Ms. Colbert, my science teacher," Chelsea explained, "she's taking us all in the van. We'll follow Shadrach in his pickup when goes looking for opossum who need help. Ms. Colbert'll pick us up and bring us home."

"Oh yeah, that sounds wonderful. Beautiful," Pop declared. "Ridin' around on a school night lookin' for the opossum. Shadrach find a lot of them, does he, little girl?"

"Yeah, he found two last time," Chelsea answered. "One had to be put down. But at least he saved it from a slow death, and that's real important too. The other one got well and got released back into the wild."

"Okay, little girl," Pop agreed, "gimme the paper you want signed. If you're gonna be with your teacher and that dude Shadrach, I got no problem. I got a lot of respect for that Shadrach. Guy come in the garage, a buddy of Shadrach's. He told me Shadrach was in Iraq during the war, and one of those IEDs exploded. Everybody in the squad died except for Shadrach. He got one of these Purple Hearts and some other medals too. But he hides them."

Pop put the permission slip on the end table and took the pen from Chelsea. "Shadrach had such an awful thing happen to him," Pop went on. "And still he reaches out to help the little animals. He takes time to teach you kids about compassion and stuff. I got nothing but admiration for the guy. You got my permission on this project one hundred percent."

Pop signed the permission slip and handed it back to Chelsea. At that moment, Mom came in. She looked as though she'd had a rough day.

"Mom," Chelsea announced, "me and my friends are going with Ms. Colbert and Shadrach Monday evening. We're gonna look for wounded opossums. It sounds really exciting."

"*What?*" Mom cried. "You're going out at night on the streets where Marko Lane was almost murdered by some madman?"

"Mom, we're gonna be out between six and ten," Chelsea explained. "Marko got hurt in the middle of the night, and, anyway, a madman probably didn't do it. Marko has lotsa enemies. He's so mean to everybody."

"You're going with that Shadrach, right?" Mom asked. "You and him and that teacher will be roaming around in the middle of the night." Mom glanced in Pop's direction. "Of course you're fine with this, right, Lorenzo?"

"Babe," Pop responded, "Shadrach's a good man. He got blasted in Iraq by an IED while he was fighting for *us*, right? He's what you call a hero. Y'hear what I'm sayin'? He's sacrificed more than I ever did. So I gotta respect the man. If it's okay with the teacher, it's okay with me. I already signed the permission slip."

"Oh, of course," Mom complained. "Who needs *my* signature? She's only my daughter."

"I know you had a hard day with the educator types today, babe," Pop told her, "but take it easy. Everything's cool."

Mom went into the kitchen to make tea. Chelsea and Pop exchanged glances. Pop shrugged, as if to say, "Don't worry. It's okay."

On the way to her room, Chelsea overheard Jaris talking on his cell in his room. She paused a minute and listened.

"Yeah, yeah," Jaris was saying. "You're okay, Trevor. You didn't do anything. Just relax. I got your back, Trev. Take it slow. You'll be in the clear in no time when they find the guy who did this."

Then Jaris ended the call, and Chelsea peeked into his room. Jaris was sprawled on his bed, and he sat up when Chelsea came in.

"Trevor?" she asked.

"Yeah, he was out jogging on Pequot Street too the night Marko got hit," Jaris answered. "The cops already questioned him."

"They couldn't blame Trevor, could they?" Chelsea asked.

"Marko's parents are putting a lot of pressure on the cops to solve this," Jaris explained. "And Marko isn't making matters any better. He says he and Trevor were fighting just before he was whacked. Marko's acting like he thinks Trevor did it."

Jaris sat there, worried sick. His thoughts turned to Kevin. Kevin hadn't seemed to care that Marko Lane had been attacked. Kevin's lack of sympathy bothered Jaris.

Kevin didn't even seem surprised. Maybe he just didn't care. That was probably it. Jaris couldn't blame him for not caring. He had made Kevin's life a nightmare. Why should Kevin worry about Marko?

Jaris knew Kevin Walker was not at home that night. His grandparents didn't know where he was. Maybe he was out running that night too. Boxers train by running. Jaris didn't want to start asking Kevin questions. Kevin was a good guy, but he was touchy. He'd learned to trust his little group of friends in Alonee's posse. If Jaris even hinted that Kevin may have had something to do with Marko's injury, Kevin might never forgive him.

At school on Monday, Kevin and Trevor attended all their classes. Jaris wanted to speak privately with Kevin's girlfriend, Carissa. He knew she usually went to the vending machine between classes to buy a banana. So when Jaris came out of English, he waited for her.

Jaris stood at the vending machine, pretending to be making a choice.

"Hi, Carissa. Everything looks good, right?" he remarked. "Usually I get an orange, but those apples look pretty terrific. I suppose you'll get your usual banana."

"You know me," Carissa replied with a laugh. "I just love bananas. They're good for you too. They got potassium. I'm not sure what that's good for, but it's good."

"Carissa," Jaris began, still looking at the vending machine. "Have you noticed that Kevin is a little edgy lately? Is everything okay with him? He flies off the handle real easy, and I don't want to hit his hot buttons."

Carissa got her banana from the machine and started peeling it. To Jaris's concern, she didn't answer right away. "Yeah," she finally answered, "I've noticed that too, Jaris. I love Kevin, but he's hard to be with sometimes. He's got this gloomy side to him, but I can usually do some dumb thing to make him laugh. But I can't lately."

She took a nibble of the banana. "Something's bugging him. I know he's really determined to follow through on this boxing stuff. And he doesn't want to tell his grandparents. They'd be really upset. They'd think he was getting like his father and pretty soon he'd be in trouble."

Kevin put his money into the machine and chose an apple. "Still," Carissa continued, "it bothers Kevin that he's keeping stuff from the grandparents. He loves them a lot, and he wants to be open with them. He's torn by that. Still, I don't know for sure if that's what's bothering him."

"I don't know, Carissa," Jaris responded. "This thing that happened to Marko Lane. Kevin reacted in a strange way. I mean, none of us like Marko. He's given us all a lot of trouble, but Kevin seemed weird about it. He seemed like he not only didn't care if Marko lived or died. He wasn't even surprised."

Carissa had been eating her banana, and now she stopped. Her eyes got very big. She looked stricken.

"Carissa," Jaris asked gently, "have you come right out and asked Kevin what's bothering him?"

"Yeah, I did, a coupla times," the girl answered. "He clammed up on me, Jaris. You know, I really care about Kevin, and he says he cares about me. But he doesn't really trust me. I hate to say that. You know, when we first started going together, we shared secrets from our lives. I told him stuff about me. Then he told me about his father that he'd never told to anybody before."

Carissa sighed and went on. "I know I talk too much, especially to my mom. I made the terrible mistake of telling my mom what Kevin told me. And Mom, she's a gossip. She told other people. I thought Kevin would never speak to me again, but he forgave me. It was my fault that the stuff about his father got out for Marko Lane to use against him."

Jaris took a bit out his apple. What Carissa was telling him was old news for him. "I felt so horrible," the girl admitted, "I wanted to die. He said he forgave me, and he was nice about it. But he doesn't completely trust me anymore. That hurts me a lot, but I guess it's my own fault. . . . Anyway, I don't know what's bothering him. He doesn't trust me enough to tell me."

"My mom talks too much to her mom too, my grandma," Jaris commented. "That causes a lot of problems in our family."

"Yeah," Carissa said. "I regret so much that I lost Kevin's confidence. I mean, when you're as close as we are, you should be able to say *anything* to each other. I feel so bad. Now when he really needs a shoulder to cry on or something, he can't turn to me."

"Maybe eventually you'll get his confidence back, Carissa," Jaris suggested.

"Or else it'll break us up," Carissa commented sadly.

# CHAPTER EIGHT

After school, Jaris went over to the track field. Trevor, Matson Malloy, Kevin, and the other boys were doing their stretches. The team had a warm camaraderie. The boys joked and teased one another like friends.

Coach Curry got them together and gave them a pep talk. It was time to get over the "summer lazies," he told them. "Some of you been laying on the beach all summer," he told them. "That's all over now. We got a tough schedule this year. As you all know, we're going without one of our best runners, Marko Lane. At this point, we don't know if he can come back or not. What we need to do is work even harder, no matter what happens."

Jaris sat on the sidelines and watched the trial runs. Kevin looked great, but Trevor was off his stride. His mind was too clogged with worry to put everything into his running. But whatever demons Kevin was dealing with, they weren't affecting his performance in the least.

Jaris waited to talk to Kevin alone. He figured the best time would be after practice. Kevin usually jogged home through the brushy fields between the school and his grandparents' little place. Today, Chelsea was riding home with Pop. So Jaris had this time free.

Jaris caught up to Kevin soon after he started for home. He jogged up alongside Kevin. "What you doin' here, man?" Kevin asked, surprised. "You following me?"

"I wanted to talk to you Kevin, just you and me," Jaris replied.

Kevin's expression hardened. His eyes narrowed. He was on the defensive these days. Of all his friends, Jaris was worried about Kevin the most. The guy had been fighting demons all his life, and sometimes they seemed to get the better of him.

"Talk about what?" Kevin asked in a hostile voice. "We got a problem that I don't know about, dude?"

"Hey man, don't treat me like I'm your enemy," Jaris responded. "We're brothers, right? I was just worried about you. You seem in a dark place. I got experience with that, with my pop and with me too. Sometimes my father used to live in a darkness that covered the whole house."

Jaris paused for a moment to catch an extra breath. "Sometimes it happens to me too," he went on. "I feel like a loser. Sometimes I think I can accomplish a lot and have a good life. Other times I think I'm fooling myself. I get outta the dumps by talking to Alonee and Sami. Or I talk to Sereeta and my pop. I'm afraid you don't talk to anybody and you're keeping things locked inside you."

Some of the hostility drained from Kevin's face. Just ahead was a makeshift place to sit. A tree felled by lightning years ago had left a log to rest on. A lot of people walking the trail took a break on that log. Now Kevin stopped at the log and sat down. He left room for Jaris.

Kevin buried his face in his hands for a few moments. Then he admitted, "It's hard to talk about stuff, man."

"I know," Jaris agreed, laying a hand briefly on Kevin's shoulder. "But one thing you can be sure of. Whatever you tell me, stays with me. I don't take anything further. You can feel safe talking to me, man. If there's anything you need to share, I'll respect your trust forever."

"I know, Jaris. You're okay," Kevin responded.

Kevin took a deep breath and started talking to his friend. "You know I'm taking those boxing lessons. When I started, I thought it'd be a good way to get rid of the anger I feel sometimes. I really enjoy boxing. But I think there's a part of me wants to learn to fight and use my hands as weapons.

Part of me wants to be able to deal with people like Marko in a violent way. When I'd hit the bag at the gym, Marko's face was on it. You know, in my mind. I thought the boxing lessons would release some of the violence I feel. But it makes it worse. It's almost like a frenzy."

"Is that what's bothering you, man?" Jaris asked.

"No," Kevin shook his head and went on. "Only part of it. It's about Lane. When you guys told me what happened to him, I was so happy. I was hoping he'd die. I really wanted him to die. I don't want to be like that, Jaris. It made me so sick that I felt that way. I'm turning into a monster."

Kevin held out his hands, palms up. He had an agonized look on his face. "Marko hurt me a lot," he said, "but he hurt a lot of you guys too. Why should I hate him so much more than the rest of you? When he hurts Sereeta, I know that tears you, man. But you're not in a smokin' rage. Why don't you fume like I do? When I first heard that Marko got whacked, I like punched the air and yelled, 'Yesss!'"

"Kevin, we all got our demons," Jaris advised. "We're all different, and our demons are different. I wanted to punch Marko out one time. Sometimes I feel hatred too. Then I remember that it's just gonna mess me up, and Marko, he couldn't care less. I think about people who love me. My parents and Sereeta. My friends, Trevor, Derrick, Oliver, the girls . . . and you, man. I think I'm not gonna let them all down by stooping to Marko's level. And then I try to laugh it off. I try to almost feel sorry for Marko 'cause it can't be fun being such an idiot."

Kevin took a deep breath. "I'd like to be more like Derrick," he wished. "That is one sweet dude. Marko's taunted and humiliated him more than anybody, and there's no hatred in that guy."

"Kevin, you can't be Derrick, and I can't either," Jaris told his friend. "But lissen up, man. Oliver Randall is one of the coolest guys I've ever known. He's like unflappable. But one day Marko came down on Oliver's dad. Marko called him a stupid old geezer or something like that. Oliver was ready to lay Marko out. There woulda been a bad fight. Remember what happened, Kev?"

Kevin nodded his head yes. "You grabbed Oliver's arm," Jaris went on. "You stopped him from making an awful mistake. He often tells me about that and how grateful he is to you. You see, Kevin, you're no monster. You didn't give in to your old rage. You had Oliver's back. You knew fighting on campus could've gotten him kicked outta school. You helped somebody else control his anger."

Kevin smiled a little. "Yeah," he admitted.

"You're more in control than you think, Kevin," Jaris assured him. "You're all right. You can't help the feelings that bubble up inside you. Look at it this way. Say you're walking down the street, and you see this cool-looking chick. Maybe you feel pretty excited. But you don't do or say anything rude or uncool. Right? So you're in control, man. Don't sell yourself short."

Kevin laughed. "Hey man, thanks," he chuckled. "Believe it or not, I feel better. I really do."

"Good!" Jaris exclaimed. "We can't have one of Alonee's posse going it alone. No way. We're in this together man. We got each other's backs."

"Hey, Jaris," he said, with his fist in the bump position, "*thanks*."

The boys fist-bumped, and Kevin went on home. Jaris turned back toward the neighborhood where he lived.

As he walked home, relief flooded Jaris's heart. For a while, he had actually wondered whether Kevin *did* have something to do with what happened to Marko. Now he was completely reassured. Kevin was the good guy Jaris always thought he was. He was just struggling with a serious temper, but he was keeping it under control.

When Jaris got home, Chelsea was happily getting ready for her opossum rescue trip. Pop wasn't home yet. Mom still looked a little unhappy about the upcoming field trip during the school year. But Shadrach being a war hero took the wind out of her sails. She was very patriotic, and she swallowed her misgivings. Still, she didn't like the thought of her daughter on a mission to rescue wounded opossums in the dark.

Mom spoke quietly to Jaris, so that Chelsea couldn't hear. She said, "For the life of me, I don't know where the child's obsession comes from. Those are hideous little animals. She never used to be that way. When she was little, we took her to the petting zoo. A poor little goat tried to make friends with her—a nice, clean little goat. Chelsea ran screaming to her father."

"Yeah, I remember that," Jaris recalled. "I was four, so she must have been two. I think I was scared of the goat too. He sorta had a beard. I thought he was a little old man on four legs."

"Now she's so enamored of these horrid opossums," Mom groaned. "You must admit, Jaris, they're ghastly creatures. If she was rescuing rabbits or something, I could understand things a little better."

"Well, maybe they'll branch out into other animals, like maybe skunks," Jaris suggested.

"Jaris," Mom chided, "I've said it before, and I'll say it again. Every day you get more like your father with his sick sense of humor. I'm not sure I can stand two of you in the same house."

"I'm sorry, Mom," Jaris apologized, hurrying to his room.

Later that night, the Chelsea and her friends were in the van with Ms. Colbert. They were in a neighborhood full of brushy vacant lots, with a few ravines. Over the years, many kinds of wildlife had adjusted to living in a built-up neighborhood by living in undeveloped pockets. There were raccoons, skunks, foxes, and opossum. Sometimes even young coyotes came into the ravines from the nearby hills. The rabbits lived nearer and nearer to the homes. At night, they raided the vegetable gardens.

"There's Shadrach," Ms. Colbert pointed. "He's going down Iroquois Street." The van followed the slow moving pickup truck. They turned down Mohican Street. When they turned onto Pequot Street, they saw a few houses and small stores. A small mini mall was at the end of the street. Pequot was also on a steep hill. That's why it was a favorite with the runners from Tubman. You could strengthen your legs there.

"Look, there's somebody pushing a shopping cart," Chelsea noted. "It looks like a lady. Is Shadrach stopping?"

"Yes," Ms. Colbert replied. "That's Tilly. She's a regular around here. Shadrach stops and gives her something. He passes out little snacks and stuff to the homeless."

"Wow, she looks old," Athena remarked. "She looks much older than my grandmother! What's she doing living on the street?"

"She has no choice," Ms. Colbert answered.

"How come?" Heston asked. "Why doesn't she live in an apartment or a room? She must get Social Security."

"She gets a very small Social Security check," Ms. Colbert explained. "If she had to pay rent, she wouldn't have anything left for food, medicine, even a pair of shoes."

They neared the ravine at the end of the street. Chelsea looked at Athena. She whispered, "This is where Marko Lane got attacked. This is where he was running."

"Yeah," Athena replied. "Is he any better?"

"He's doing okay," Chelsea answered. "Mrs. Lennox, Alonee's mother, she said he might get out of the hospital in a few days."

Shadrach pulled to a stop near the ravine. The van stopped behind him, and everyone got out. When Shadrach got out, he told them about the ravine. "Lotta times we find wounded opossum down there. Sometimes they'll take refuge there when a dog is chasing them. They get up the trees and escape sometimes, but often they've already been bitten. That's where we come in."

The two adults and four teenagers gathered at the top of the ravine. "Wow, look at the mess down there," Chelsea remarked. "Somebody dumped all their garbage, and it looks awful."

Shadrach had a powerful flashlight, and he swept the beam into the ravine. "Hey," he noted, "that's an overturned shopping cart. Belongs to one of the homeless guys. He must have lost control of it at the steep part of Pequot. It came flying down here."

Turning to the others, he said, "I'm going down to investigate. I can sometimes recognize the shopping carts. I know most of the homeless people. Maybe I can figure out who that belongs to."

"Can we come, too?" Chelsea asked.

"Yeah, but watch your step," Shadrach cautioned.

Chelsea, Athena, Heston, and Maurice followed Shadrach, but Ms. Colbert remained on top.

"Yeah," Shadrach commented. "Look, everything the poor guy had in the world is right here. It's Akron's stuff. I'm sure of it. Akron used to work on cars in Detroit. He lost his job, his family. He drifted out west and ended up here. He collects those freebie auto sales books from in front of the deli. See them scattered around? And I gave him some tuna fish packets and puddings. Here they are. He likes lemon chiffon, so I got him those. See, right here?"

"I wonder what happened?" Maurice asked. "Is he an old guy? Maybe he got a heart attack."

"He's about seventy," Shadrach explained. "He's been in the hospital a few times. Turned to booze, and that didn't help. He was in a group home. But he didn't like the fighting that goes on in some of those places. So he moved to the streets. Those little tuna fish cartons are good 'cause you get the small can of tuna, even a tiny spoon, and some crackers. It doesn't need refrigeration. Akron loves tuna fish. You can keep them in the shopping cart and just pop them open when you're hungry. Works out real good. But there's a lot of the tuna fish packets and pudding cups here. I passed them out a coupla days ago. Looks like he hadn't the chance to use much of it before he had this accident."

"That's nice you do that, Shadrach," Chelsea remarked.

"Yeah well, the homeless, they're sort like the opossum in a way," Shadrach explained. "They're outcasts. Regular folks are turned off by opossum and homeless people. They're not pretty."

Shadrach's eyebrows became furrowed. "This worries me," he commented. "I wonder where the poor guy is? I don't like seeing this little bit of blood on the cart."

"You think he's laying around here dead somewhere?" Heston asked nervously.

"We'd smell something, I think," Shadrach replied.

"If he lost his stuff," Maurice suggested, "you'd think he would've come down here to get it back. I'd sure come get my stuff if it went over a ravine."

"He's got arthritis, Maurice," Shadrach explained. "He could never make it down here. His legs are stiff. He can hardly walk. He'd never make it down here like we did. When you're able-bodied, you take it for granted that you can go anywhere you want. But a lotta folks can't. We're the lucky ones, Maurice."

Chelsea looked at Shadrach with fresh admiration. He considered himself lucky. He wasn't wasting a minute lamenting the lost eye, the damaged cheek. He was grateful to be alive and able.

"Should we try to put it back together for him?" Chelsea asked.

"Yeah, as much as we can," Shadrach agreed. He returned to his pickup truck and brought back some plastic bags. He and the teenagers retrieved the food, the T-shirts and underwear, and the auto books, along with Akron's water bottles. They put them all neatly in the bags. But the shopping cart was trashed. When it had flown over the edge, it hit a rock outcrop very hard. It was now broken and beyond repair. "I'll just toss this in my pickup and turn it over to a recycler," Shadrach said.

Just before they were about to leave the ravine, Maurice shouted, "I see something white over there behind that tree."

"Let's take a look," Shadrach suggested.

They all trooped over to find a cowering opossum with a broken leg. The beady-eyed little creature saw the people approaching.

It tried desperately to drag itself away, but it was no use.

"Don't be scared, little fella," Shadrach said in a gentle voice. "We're gonna help you."

"I'm glad you saw him, Maurice," Chelsea remarked.

"You bet!" Shadrach agreed, smiling at the boy. "Good job, Maurice."

"Oh!" Athena cried. "That's why the blood is on the shopping cart. I bet when the shopping cart crashed over the edge into the ravine, it hit this little guy."

"Sounds like that's just what happened," Shadrach responded. He got a cage from the pickup and brought it down for the opossum. Then he looked at Maurice and spoke to him. "Let me tell you something, boy. If you hadn't spotted this little guy, he would have died. He'd lay down here, slowly dying for maybe a week. No food, no water. Look at how his leg is twisted. He must be in so much pain."

Shadrach was looking Maurice in the eye. "You saved him, Maurice. Don't you ever forget it. You're only fourteen, and you got a long life ahead of you. You'll do a lot of great stuff, but don't you ever forget what you did tonight. You stopped suffering."

Maurice tried to act cool. He shrugged his shoulders. But Chelsea could see something in his eyes that she had never seen before. He was tough, and he didn't like to show a soft side. But he was proud right now. Chelsea thought that Shadrach had no idea how much his praise meant to the boy. Maurice came from a large, busy family. His parents were too poor and too stressed to spend much time nurturing Maurice.

They drove back to the opossum rescue center, where they watched Shadrach take care of the animal. He set the opossum's broken leg, gave it pain medication, and put it gently on a blanket. He set out food and water. The opossum was lying quietly as they got ready to leave.

"Well, all we need to do now is find Akron and make sure he's okay," Shadrach announced. "I'd like to give him back some of his stuff. But that's not gonna be easy. What happened has got to have been traumatic for him, and he's probably hiding somewhere."

The teenagers waited in the van while Ms. Colbert said goodnight to Shadrach by his pickup truck. The students heard Shadrach say something and Ms. Colbert's soft, tinkling laughter. They saw the two grin and chat. Then the man and woman drew closer, and finally they kissed each other good-bye. Ms. Colbert returned to the van, her face radiant. "Well, we had quite a night," she declared. "And I'll have you guys home before ten."

# CHAPTER NINE

You guys!" Chelsea squealed as she bounded into the house. "We had just an amazing time. It was exciting and sad and happy. I got loads of stuff for my science journal. You know what? Being in the opossum rescue program is the best thing ever!"

Mom and Pop were sitting in the living room. Pop was using a laptop computer to do his accounting for the garage. Mom was on her computer, creating a test for her class. Jaris was reading one of the books required for AP American History.

"Slow down, little girl," Pop laughed. "What happened?"

Chelsea rushed over and sat on the arm of her father's chair. "We rescued a poor opossum with a broken leg. A homeless man's shopping cart musta came flying down that steep hill on Pequot Street. And we think it hit the opossum. Shadrach brought it back to the refuge and helped it. We all watched him do it. It was so cool."

Pop nodded approvingly. Mom listened intently. "And that's all," Chelsea rattled on. "This guy Akron, it was his shopping cart. He lost everything he had in the whole world, even the food Shadrach gave him. Shadrach gives tuna fish and puddings that don't need refrigeration to all the homeless people. So we picked up some of the food and put it in garbage bags. Now Shadrach's looking for Akron, but he's probably hiding 'cause he's really sick."

Pop laughed again. "Monie, did you get any of that?"

"No," Mom answered, smiling against her will. "Sweetie, who's Akron?"

Jaris spoke up. "He's one of the homeless guys who push these shopping carts around. When he was young, he worked in a car factory in Detroit. Then he made tires in Akron, and he got this nickname. He's one of the regulars in the streets and alleys."

Mom looked alarmed. She turned to her son and asked, "Jaris, how do you know so much about this man?"

"Oh," Jaris explained, "sometimes when I'm walking home from school, he's there. He's always asking for change for a cup of coffee. I give him whatever I have in my pocket. I guess he doesn't get to talk much. So once he told me all about his life, and it was pretty sad. He was doing okay, belonged to a union and stuff."

Jaris put the bookmark in his book and closed it. "Then we stopped making so many cars, you know. He was one of the workers laid off. He had a wife and four children, but he hasn't seen any of them in over twenty years. When he started drinking hard, the wife took off with the kids.

Akron isn't a bad man. He's just one of life's biggest losers."

Chelsea chimed in. "Shadrach, he gets these tuna fish packets and little plastic pudding cups. It's all stuff that doesn't have to be kept cold. Then he passes them out to homeless people like Akron. Shadrach has such a big heart. Anyway, poor Akron musta lost control of his shopping cart on that steep part of Pequot Street. It went flyin' into the ravine, and all his stuff was scattered."

"How come he didn't go get it back," Mom asked.

"Oh," Chelsea explained, "he's got weak legs. He can't climb down and get his stuff. I bet Akron is huddled in some alley, real hungry. I bet he's wishing he had some of that tuna fish and pudding. Shadrach's looking for him."

"Boy," Jaris remarked, "these homeless people hang on to their shopping carts for dear life. I wonder how he lost control of it?"

"Maybe he got a heart attack or something," Chelsea suggested. "Maybe he's in the hospital now. . . . Oh, and another thing. Maurice is a jerk sometimes, but it was him who spotted the wounded opossum. Shadrach praised him so much, Maurice like just glowed. I think working with Shadrach and the opossums is gonna be so good for Maurice."

Mom was still thinking about Jaris's encounters with Akron. "Jaris," she advised, "you really shouldn't be talking to those homeless people. They could be dangerous. I know you feel sorry for them, and that's a good thing. But there are agencies that help them. Individual people shouldn't mess with them because you could get hurt. Many of them are, you know, crazy."

"Hey!" Pop piped up. "Remember that dude in the Bible, that guy who fell among the robbers and was left bleedin' by the side of the road? Good thing that fool come along, the one they call the Good Samaritan. I mean, that was dangerous, pickin' up that guy. That Samaritan dude was pretty stupid to get involved, right? I bet they had agencies in those days too. Only trouble is, agencies don't all the time work out. Then you gotta have ordinary people reachin' out."

Mom glared at her husband. "I hear what you're saying, Lorenzo," she granted. "But you've got to admit some of those homeless people are dangerous. They could suddenly freak out and attack someone."

"You know what, you guys?" Jaris said slowly. "I'm having a weird thought. You think Akron's shopping cart flying down Pequot Street could be connected with Marko getting attacked there? I mean, I'm not sure how they might be connected. But it seems odd they both happened on Pequot Street."

"Maybe Akron saw what happened to Marko," Chelsea cried. "Maybe he was a witness! He maybe got so upset when he saw some guy hitting Marko with a baseball bat. Then he just let go of his shopping cart on that steep hill. I bet that's what happened!"

"You might have something there, chili pepper," Jaris responded. "Akron's a very frightened man, always jumping at shadows. That'd be enough to scare him so bad that he abandoned his shopping cart and ran for cover. Man, wouldn't that be great if Akron was a witness? Then poor Trevor wouldn't have to be living this nightmare anymore."

"I hope Shadrach finds Akron real quick," Chelsea remarked. "I'm gonna text Shad and tell him what we think. When he finds Akron, he can ask him about what happened."

At school on Tuesday, Jaris met Sami and Alonee at the Harriet Tubman statue. He asked them how their visit with Marko went.

"Not so good," Alonee reported. "His father was there. He looked at us like we were a big conspiracy to hurt Marko. His dad just stared at us with hate in his eyes. He thinks we put Marko in the hospital, and we're glad it happened. He thinks everybody at Tubman hated Marko 'cause his father is rich and gives him stuff. Mr. Lane says it's all jealousy."

"Yeah, that's right," Sami added. "My parents and Alonee's parents brought flowers and one of these get-well balloons. But Marko, he just glare at us, like we all a bunch of hypocrites. His father, he sittin' there with his arms folded like he's guarding Marko. He like thinkin' one of us come in there to finish his boy off."

Sami shook her head in disbelief. "Those are weird people," she went on. "Y'hear what I'm sayin'? Mr. Lane, he lookin' at that poor red balloon like it's gonna explode and blow everyone up or somethin'. He made us take the balloon back."

Jasmine Benson, Marko's girlfriend, was going by and overheard Sami speaking.

# CHAPTER NINE

"You ought to be ashamed, Jaris Spain," Jasmine cried. "You and all the others who treated Marko so bad."

Jaris rolled his eyes. "Jasmine," he responded, "Marko treated us all like dirt. You know it. Any time somebody had a bad day, or trouble at home, there was Marko. He loved taunting people. We've put up with so much from that guy. He's the biggest bully and pain who ever went to this school. And you know it, Jasmine."

"He almost died, Jaris, and you're talking trash about him!" Jasmine yelled. "What's wrong with you, boy, you got no heart?"

Sami Archer tried to change the subject. "When's Marko gonna be able to come back to school, Jaz?" she asked.

"Why you askin', Sami?" Jasmine snapped bitterly. "You got a welcome party planned? Maybe people dropping bricks off the roof of the school as he goes by? Or maybe everybody could line up with baseball bats to make sure they get the job done?"

"We just wanted to maybe invite him over for pizza. We could tell him we're glad he's back," Alonee answered calmly.

"Sister," Jasmine cried shrilly, "are you kiddin' me? You'd all poison his pizza! You think me and Marko some kind of fools? He got all your numbers, dudes. He knows what he's up against around here now. But Marko Lane, he's no coward. He's coming back here to Tubman. He's gonna hold his head high. He's gonna defy all you creeps to try to take him down again."

Jasmine looked around at the small group. She was speaking so loudly that even students passing by could hear her. "This time he's on to you. He's woke up that you won't stop at nothin' 'cause he's handsome and smart and charming. None of you can hold a candle to him. The only way you can beat him is with a baseball bat!"

"Jasmine," Jaris suggested, "soak your head in some ice water. Maybe the shock will get you some common sense and reality. I don't know who attacked Marko, but it wasn't any of us. It wasn't any of my friends. Marko's such a freakin' mean dude that most of us hate his guts, but we would not harm him. We're not that kind of people, Jasmine. Do you really believe that one of us whacked Marko? 'Cause if do, then you gotta believe that little green men are landing tonight from the mother ship."

Jasmine ignored Jaris. "Was probably that fool, Trevor Jenkins," she ranted. "Trevor can't get over it that Marko can blow right past him at the track meets. Trevor's such a loser. Marko's handsomer and smarter than Trevor, and Marko can get any chick he wants. I'm so proud I'm the one he loves. The police even came around and talked to Trevor. He was out running on Pequot Street that night. Even the police think he did it, but they ain't got enough evidence yet."

That wasn't enough of an accusation for Jasmine. "But Trevor," she declared, "he's too dumb to plan this by himself. You all put him up to it. None of you man enough to face Marko eyeball to eyeball. 'Cause you know he'd beat you. No, you gotta take him out like dirty yellow cowards. You hadda sneak up on him from behind."

"Trevor had nothing to do with it," Jaris protested. "He just happened to be running on Pequot Street the same night as Marko."

"Marko told the cops what he thinks," Jasmine told them. "And they were mighty interested. They already questioned the sucka, and he didn't impress them much. He was all shaky and guilty looking. I think they're building their case, and they gonna be closin' in real soon. This whole rotten scheme to hurt Marko is gonna blow sky-high. You all gonna be caught in the back-lash. It ain't just gonna be that fool Jenkins goin' down. He's gonna take his whole gang with him."

"Oh brother!" Jaris groaned. "What an idiot!"

"You be afraid, Jaris Spain. You be very much afraid," Jasmine warned. "You be sweatin' 'cause trying to murder somebody ain't no little thing." She turned and strode away.

The group was stunned into silence for a moment. Then Sami spoke.

"That's about how it went down at the hospital," she remarked. "We were tryin' to be nice and sympathetic. Some people, you just can't make peace with."

Alonee shook her head sadly, "My mom was really hurt by how the Lanes acted," she commented.

"I dread Marko coming back thinking we were all behind the attack," Jaris admitted. "He was bad before. What's he gonna be like when he thinks we all tried to murder him?"

"If only the police could find who really did it," Alonee hoped.

"Maybe somebody in that Anderson family, the people Marko's father cheated," Sami suggested. "You remember how bitter Shatara was? She was so happy about Marko dying in the hospital. His dad caused an awful misery in that family.

Maybe the old grandfather ain't as demented as they think. Maybe he know he let himself get cheated outta the property he'd promised the kids. Maybe he decided to take Marko out."

"I'm wondering, though," Jaris asked, "could an old man swing a bat hard enough to injure Marko like that?"

"I think so," Alonee replied. "The blow didn't have to be that strong for a laceration and a concussion. If Marko had been hit hard, he would've had a major concussion and maybe bleeding in the brain. His skull could've even been broken. He could've died right away. Whoever swung the bat could've been an older person or even a woman. A strong young guy probably would have done him in."

The outlines for AP American History had been turned in last Friday. Today, Ms. McDowell was returning them with her comments. The central question for the course was defining how important supreme court decisions of the past century had influenced American life.

Jaris had worked hard on his outline, but he dreaded Ms. McDowell's opinion. She had said that she would be brutally honest in the first evaluation. Things could go two ways, she explained. The outlines would show that the student would be able to succeed in the course. Otherwise, she would advise dropping out and taking something less demanding.

"This class is going to take a lot of your time," Ms. McDowell had warned. "That time may be better spent on other challenging senior classes. So if you have little chance of getting college credit, I'm going to tell you that early."

Jaris walked nervously into the classroom. Ms. McDowell was already there, with the stack of corrected outlines on her desk. Jaris got pains in his stomach just thinking about the teacher's comments. He glanced over at Oliver Randall. The guy was a genius. He didn't have to worry about doing well. Sereeta was smart too, but all the turmoil in her family might have affected her work. Jaris felt sorry for her. Alonee always did well, so she'd be all right. Jaris figured he'd end up on the bottom of the heap, even if he made the cut.

Before returning the outlines, Ms. McDowell made an announcement. "I told you that I thought all of you were capable of gaining college credit," she said. "However, some of you did not turn in a very promising outline. You went on the Internet and produced a hastily thrown-together bunch of facts. A few of you chose poor Web sites as well, and I found serious errors in your outlines. Having said all that, I'll return your outlines and let you decide whether you want to stay in the course."

Jaris's feelings shot back down the same old dark corridors he'd often traveled in his mind. A mocking little voice that he knew too well warned him that he had overstepped his limits. He was not AP American History material. He was not up to the job. He was the clumsy kid trying out for the major leagues when he could hardly cut it in the minors.

Jaris tried to console himself. It would not be the end of the world if Ms. McDowell gave him discouraging comments. But he wanted very much to do well. Making the AP course would be such a boost to his dreams of doing well in college and having a teaching career.

When Jaris got his outline back, he steeled himself against the criticism. But he blinked when he read the scrawled comments Ms. McDowell had written.

"An excellent start, Jaris! Way to go!"

Jaris rocked back in his seat, his spirits soaring.

As low as Jaris could go when doubts assailed him, that's how high he could go when he was successful. The little worry bird fluttering around in his soul rose up and flew away.

"You got a big smile on your face, dude," Oliver commented as they walked out.

"Yeah," Jaris answered, "she sorta liked my outline."

"You're good, Jaris," Oliver told his friend, "better than you think."

The rest of the day went well, but nothing could compare with Ms. McDowell's compliment. Jaris endured his math and other classes.

# CHAPTER TEN

Between classes, Jaris heard his cell phone ring and answered it. Students couldn't talk on the phone in class, but between classes they could keep their phones on.

Jaris wasn't familiar with the voice on the phone. He heard, "Is this Jaris Spain, Chelsea's brother?"

"Yeah," Jaris replied, gripping the phone tighter. He was still elated by what Ms. McDowell wrote on his outline. Now fear shot through him. What was this strange phone call about?

"This is Shadrach, Jaris," the voice said. "I think we met out on the road one day. I was holding a wounded opossum in my arms. I was pretty impressed when you shook hands with me."

Jaris didn't know what to say. There was an awkward pause in the conversation.

"Anyway," Shadrach went on, "Chelsea called me the other night. She wanted to know if I caught up to that homeless man, Akron. He lost his cart on Pequot Street the other night. She said I should ask him if he knows anything about that Tubman kid getting hit with the baseball bat. She said you thought the two incidents might be somehow connected.

Jaris waited in silence. "Well," Shadrach continued, "I've found Akron. I got him into a rescue mission. He's in terrible shape. They'll only keep him here for a few days. But I figured you might know more about that attack than I do. Maybe you'd like to come with me after school and talk to Akron."

"Yeah, I would like that, Shadrach. Thanks," Jaris responded. "I'm done with classes now, and I'm going home."

"Okay Jaris, I'll be over to your house in about thirty minutes. I'll pick you up. Is that good?" Shadrach asked.

"That'd be great," Jaris said, excitement rising in him. "I just need to get Chelsea home and I'm ready to roll." He thought this just might explain what happened to Marko Lane. Akron probably saw it all happen.

Jaris didn't tell Chelsea about the phone call from Shadrach. He thought she might want to come along too. And Jaris didn't know how impaired Akron was. He didn't want Chelsea to see something scary. So Jaris hurried from the Spain house when he saw Shadrach's pickup out front. Chelsea was busy texting in her room, telling all her friends what happened during the day.

"I appreciate this a lot, Shadrach," Jaris said.

"No problem. So tell me about what happened," Shadrach asked.

"The guy who was attacked on Pequot Street is Marko Lane," Jaris explained, "He's a creep, and a lot of people at Tubman hate him, including me and my friends. But nobody'd never hurt him. Marko and his girlfriend and his family all think the kids at Tubman plotted the attack. One of my friends was out jogging the night Marko got hit. He's been questioned by the police and everything. He's so scared he'll be blamed. I sure hope this Akron can clear things up."

Shadrach nodded. "Akron was saying a lot of weird things when I talked to him. Maybe you can connect the dots."

"You know, Shadrach," Jaris commented, "you got no idea how much this opossum rescue deal means to Chelsea. I haven't seen her this excited about anything in a long time. She just loves it."

"Chelsea's a great kid," Shadrach replied. "I like the whole group, but she's special. She's a little pistol, and she's compassionate and sweet too. You guys must have great parents. They're sure raising good kids."

"Thanks," Jaris responded. "Mom and Pop aren't perfect, but they're pretty wonderful."

They drove in silence for a minute or so.

"I found Akron hiding out in a packing case behind the bowling alley," Shadrach stated. "He hadn't eaten in a couple of days. He was so weak. He was crying. He's really a sad case, Jaris. He wondered if I had any of those tuna packets with me, and I did. He ate three of them in a row. He was ravenous."

"Do you think he maybe saw what happened, Shadrach?" Jaris asked.

"I kinda think he *knows* what happened, Jaris," Shadrach asserted.

They drove about eight miles to a small stucco house with a sign in front: "Mission."

"People here keep going on donations," Shadrach explained. "They take in desperate cases for a few days. Homeless people get a chance to shower, wash their clothes, sleep in a real bed. Lotta demand for places like this. But with governments running short of money, it's gonna have to be more private places like this."

Jaris liked Shadrach. He liked him that first afternoon when he was rescuing that bloody opossum. Jaris had an instinct for good people. He wasn't often wrong.

They pulled into the small parking area and walked to the door. A middle-aged man let them in. He seemed well acquainted with Shadrach. He led them down a hallway to a small bedroom. The place was spare, but clean.

A withered man sat in a chair beside the bed. He wore a baseball cap with the Cleveland Indians logo. Long straggly gray hair poked out from the cap. The man looked up when Shadrach and Jaris came in.

"Hello Shad," he said softly. Then he looked at Jaris. Jaris had often given him a dollar. He nodded at Jaris.

"Akron," Shadrach greeted, sitting down in one of the two folding chairs in the room. Jaris took the other.

"Akron," Jaris asked, "the other night something happened on Pequot Street. Could you talk to us about that?"

The man lowered his head. He began crying. He wiped the tears away with his sleeve. "My shopping cart," he mumbled barely above a whisper.

"Yeah, it rolled down Pequot Street and went into the ravine," Shadrach confirmed.

"Everything was in there, Shad," Akron said sadly. "My clothes, my books. Everything you gave me. I got nothing else."

"We went down and saved most of it," Shadrach assured him. "We got it in bags."

"It was all I had in this whole stinkin' world," Akron repeated.

"I know," Shadrach affirmed, putting a gentle hand on the man's shoulder.

"He was runnin'," Akron said.

"Who was running?" Jaris asked.

"This kid," Akron replied. "My shopping cart was in his way. He yelled at me. He said, 'Get your freakin' cart outta my way.' I grabbed for my cart, but he pushed it. He pushed it into the ravine on purpose. It was all I had in the whole world. Sometimes guys try to steal it. I don't let them. I got nothin' else. I keep a baseball bat to defend myself and my cart."

Jaris turned numb but said nothing.

"I grabbed for my cart," Akron went on. "But he give it such a shove, it was moving now. It's a hill there, y'know. When something's rolling there, you can't stop it. He give it a good shove, to get it outta his way, see? I tried to run after it, but it just went faster and faster. The kid, he was gone. He didn't care. All I had left was the baseball bat."

"Go on, Akron," Shadrach urged him.

"I sat on the curb and I cried," Akron admitted. "I didn't have nothin' left. It was all gone. And then he come back, runnin' like before. He didn't even look at me. He didn't see me. He was jus' running."

Akron looked at Shadrach and Jaris, as if wondering whether he should go on.

"I got up as he went by," Akron went on. "And I hit him with the baseball bat 'cause he took everything I had in the world from me. I hit him in the back of his head. He falls down, and he's bleedin'. I killed him. I run away best I could. I hid behind the bowling alley where you found me, Shad."

Akron was staring at the floor as he spoke. "They can come and git me now, Shad. I got it coming to me. I hit the kid 'cause he gave my cart a shove and I couldn't stop it. It was all I had in the world."

Shadrach looked at Jaris. There was deep sadness in both their faces.

"Akron, the boy you hit isn't dead. He's in the hospital, and he's going to be okay," Shadrach assured him.

"Yeah," Jaris affirmed, "he's gonna be out of the hospital real soon."

"You're lyin'," Akron protested.

"No!" Shadrach said. "I've never lied to you, Akron. Never. The kid is going to be okay."

Akron buried his face in his hands and sat there sobbing, oblivious to his surroundings. Jaris and Shadrach went out into the hall.

"I'll drive you home, Jaris," Shadrach said. "Then I'll come back here. I'll take care of telling the police. I know some of the cops real well. These are guys who understand this population, the mentally ill, the outcasts. They handle them with compassion."

"What'll happen to the guy?" Jaris asked.

"He's mentally ill," Shadrach replied. "The public defender'll probably plead diminished capacity. Akron'll probably go into some hospital. He won't like that, but they'll take care of him. At least he won't be out there on the street."

Shadrach glanced into the room while he spoke. "But it'll be sad for him. Most of them in the street, they want to be free. Like the opossums. It isn't about room and board. It's about freedom. They want the sky overhead and the earth beneath their feet. But there's no way out for him. He could've killed that kid. He needs care."

Shadrach told the man at the mission to keep an eye on Akron until he got back. Then Shadrach drove Jaris home.

The minute they were out of the small lot, Jaris called Trevor.

"Trevor, you're in the clear," Jaris told his friend.

"What are you talkin' about, man? Is this for real?" Trevor gasped.

"Yeah, we found this homeless man who whacked Marko that night," Jaris explained. "Marko got mad that his shopping cart was in his way and he sent it flying into a ravine. The cart had everything the guy owned. The man was so upset he beaned Marko."

"How come Marko never told the cops about that?" Trevor asked.

"He probably didn't know, Trev," Jaris replied. "He shoved the cart and then ran on. He never saw it fly into the ravine. When he came down Pequot Street again, he never saw this homeless guy with the baseball bat. Marko probably didn't think the incident was important enough to mention. Marko's that kind of a dude, Trev. He doesn't think anything of shoving a guy's shopping cart down a hill—with everything he owns in it."

"Oh man!" Trevor sighed. "You sure he did it?"

"Yeah, Trevor," Jaris assured him. "He told us the whole story. He's been in hiding ever since. He thought he'd killed Marko."

"Oh man, Jaris," Trevor said, sounding relieved. "Thanks for lettin' me know. I've been livin' in a nightmare. Wait'll I tell Ma. I gotta call Vanessa too. She's been really freakin'."

"We can thank Shadrach for solving this," Jaris told him. "He and Chelsea and the other kids found the busted shopping cart off Pequot Street. If they hadn't, we might never have known what happened. Akron, the homeless guy, woulda probably just died in the shipping crate where he was hiding. The truth would have died with him."

"I owe you and Shadrach and Chelsea," Trevor said.

"No problem, man." Jaris closed the phone.

"Shadrach, this is such a relief," Jaris sighed. "This Marko Lane's family was sure the kids at Tubman did it to him. He's such a freakin' creep that we all hate him."

"What's this guy's problem?" Shadrach asked.

"I don't know," Jaris half groaned. "He just likes to bully people. He's good looking, smart, athletic. He's got a great looking chick, although she's a creep too. I don't know what makes him tick."

"Must be a heckuva guy," Shadrach commented. "He pushes a homeless guy's shopping cart out of the way on a hill and never gives it a thought. That tells you something. To the homeless, the shopping carts are their life. Anyone with half a heart would have chased the cart and retrieved it, or at least tried. Even if he couldn't, maybe he could go down there and get the stuff back for the poor guy."

As Shadrach pulled into the Spain driveway, Jaris turned to him. "Thanks for everything, man. I really admire you. And Chelsea, she thinks you're a superhero. I guess you are. Chelsea couldn't love you more if you were some freakin' rock star."

Shadrach laughed and waved as Jaris left the car and went up the walk.

Jaris told his parents and Chelsea all that had happened out at the Mission. "Turns out," Jaris concluded, "Marko Lane was just being himself on Pequot Street. He was running. Nothing was supposed to break his stride. Then the guy and his shopping cart got in his way. Marko, he gave the cart a shove and never looked back. Marko cared so little about the guy, he never even mentioned him to the cops."

"Oh my goodness!" Mom gasped. "What a tragedy! And when I think how Marko's mother talked to me when I called her. She made it seem as though poor Marko was the victim of a big conspiracy hatched by my son and his friends. She couldn't understand how her lovable little boy could be so mistreated by all those evil students at Tubman."

"You know, Mom," Jaris said, "Trevor Jenkins was really under suspicion 'cause he was there that night. The cops questioned him and everything. What if Shadrach and the kids"—Jaris smiled at Chelsea—"hadn't found the busted shopping cart? This crime might never have been solved. Poor Trevor might have been arrested, or at least he would have lived under a cloud. So Shadrach and his little gang of opossum kids aren't only rescuing opossum. In this case, they rescued Trevor, an innocent guy."

"I knew Shadrach was wonderful," Chelsea chirped with great emotion. "He's one of the best people in the whole world."

Mom smiled weakly and agreed. "Yes, he is a very good person. And I must say I did misjudge this whole opossum thing."

"Hear! Hear!" Pop crowed with a big grin.

"Don't rub it in," Mom warned. "Just don't rub it in, Lorenzo."

"I feel sorry for the pool old dude, this Akron," Pop remarked. "Seems unfair to even punish the guy. Maybe bopping Marko Lane over the head might have a good effect on his character. Maybe they ought to give the old dude a prize."

At Tubman High the next morning, Jaris dropped Chelsea off and started toward the statue of Harriet Tubman. On his way, he saw Jasmine Benson.

"You heard?" he asked Jasmine.

"Uh yeah," the girl mumbled. "The police, they called the Lanes. They . . . uh . . .

arrested some crazy old man who attacked Marko for no reason." Jasmine seemed very subdued.

"Did the police tell you why he hit Marko?" Jaris probed. "Did they mention that this homeless man's shopping cart got in Marko's way, and he gave it a shove? Did they say how it flew down the street into a ravine? Everything the man had was in that cart, and he whacked Marko for doing that."

"Yeah, they said something about a shopping cart and stuff," Jasmine murmured. "I mean, Marko didn't know. These shopping carts get away from you real fast."

"Does Marko know about the arrest?" Jaris asked.

"Well, yeah," the girl replied. Jasmine's voice was flat and limp, like a balloon without air. "The police told him and his parents. He's comin' home tomorrow. He's doin' good. Uh . . . he says thanks to the ones who, you know, visited and called and stuff. Marko, he said he didn't even remember the old homeless man."

Jaris turned to go then, but her voice stopped him. "Jaris!" she called to him. "I'm sorry."

"What about Marko?" Jaris asked. "He sorry too?"

Jasmine didn't answer.

"Okay," Jaris responded.

"Jaris," Jasmine went on in a shaky voice. "But sorry. From me. Sorry, okay?"

Jaris nodded and went on to class.

As he walked away, Jaris tried to make sense of what happened in the past week.

That poor guy, Akron, was only trying to get by from day to day. But he was just a homeless guy—an outcast in most people's eyes. Marko didn't even remember him.

"Why do we do that?" Jaris asked himself. "Why do we make outcasts of innocent people and innocent creatures?"

Shadrach helped Akron, as he helped the opossums. And he helped the algebra students at school. In Shadrach's world, there were no outcasts. He embraced everyone and everything.

But that was because Shadrach was an outcast himself, like the opossums he rescued. For many people, Shadrach's injuries set him apart. And the opossums were only unwanted pests. Even Mom wasn't so sure about him and his opossums. Inessa, Chelsea's friend, wanted no part of them. Only Chelsea accepted him and his program for what they were.

Then Jaris thought about Marko. "Oh yeah!" he thought with a smirk on his face. "Then there's Marko. He doesn't need anyone to make him an outcast. He takes care of that all by himself."

Jaris was sitting down in his next class by this time. But one more thought came to mind: We could all be better people if we were more like Shadrach.